Pierce

MCCRAY BRUIN BOOK 5

KATHI S. BARTON

World Castle Publishing, LLC
Pensacola, Florida
Copyright © Kathi S. Barton 2021
Paperback ISBN: 9781953271815
eBook ISBN: 9781953271822
First Edition World Castle Publishing, LLC, February 22, 2021
http://www.worldcastlepublishing.com
Licensing Notes
Cover: Karen Fuller
Editor: Maxine Bringenberg

Prologue

"Joey, there's a call for you." She turned and looked at the man she'd hired just yesterday to answer calls for her. "He said it's important he speaks with you now."

"Tell him to fuck off." Turning back to the work she was doing, she knew that Harvey, her secretary, wasn't going to last the day if he didn't stop bothering her with little shit. "Well? Did you tell him?"

"No. He said he'd have to have the police come here if you didn't want to hear what he has to say. I'm not sure telling him to fuck off is such a good idea." She stomped toward him. "Don't hurt me."

That stopped her dead in her tracks. She'd never hurt anyone. Joey knew she had a volatile temper, but she never hurt people. Telling Harvey she was sorry for snapping at him, she picked up the phone and gave the idiot who called her today all she wanted to in the way of anger.

"You had fucking better have your ducks in a row, you uneducated couch potato. I'm working in the event no one told you. What the fuck do you want?" His laughing wasn't something she thought was helping. "I'm hanging up now. If you ever call here again, I will —"

"Your niece, Rebecca Hightower, has been murdered." Joey slid to the floor, her legs suddenly no longer strong enough to hold her up. She asked the man if her husband had done it. "At this point, we're only *assuming* he did. Not that he was the one that pulled the trigger, but I think you understand what might have happened. Her daughter, Becky, is staying with my family. Becky told me I wasn't to trust your sister, Margaret, with any information."

"No. Don't call her. She and Peter are close. I think she is still having an affair with him despite him being married to Rebecca. Where are you?" Ian told her his name as well as where they were. "And Becky? Is she hurt too? It wouldn't be any sweat off his balls to kill his own child."

"She's fine. Scared out of her mind. The doctor told us she was dehydrated and malnourished. We're taking care that she is getting plenty of food and water. Rebecca is tagged as a Jane Doe for now. The police are friends of the family and have taken precautions to make sure no one knows of her death or that she was found. Becky told my daughter that her father would kill us all if he were to find us helping her."

"More than likely, he would. He's not the best of

people to be around." Joey thought of all the things she knew about Peter. "I'd like to come and see Becky if you think it'll be safe. I don't want her hurt either. She and Rebecca have been through a great deal while she was married to that fat fuck."

"You certainly have a way with words." She laughed with him. "If you don't mind me saying so, I thought that with you being Becky's great aunt, you'd be — at least sound a little older. You can't be much older than Rebecca was."

"We're all three the same age. Margie and I are twins. Rebecca is my older brother's daughter. He was only sixteen when he got this girl, Sheila, pregnant. Mom had just found out that she was going to have us. It was a race, Mom used to tell us, to see who delivered first. We were born a day earlier than Rebecca. My brother committed suicide about a week after his child was born." Ian told her he was sorry. "Me too. I have no idea why I'm telling you this. You more than likely have a lot of things going on there too. Anyway, I'm not going to be coming there until I hear from you. Also, call me on my cell phone from now on. If you call and I don't answer, it's because I'm working. But I will return your call if you leave me a message."

After giving him the phone number, she told him she wanted to speak to Becky if she could. Ian told her he'd make sure she called her back when he returned home tonight. She was staying with his wife and her sisters.

"Christ, man. How do you live in a house full of women? You must be the most patient person in the world to be able to do that." Ian laughed, and she had to smile. He had a good laugh, one she thought she'd like to hear more often. "Just keep me updated, please. And when the time is right, I'll tell my sister. She's a pain in the ass most of the time, so I won't subject you to that. Also, if you could tell Becky I love her, that would be great. Thanks for telling me, Ian. I'm sorry you're involved in this. But I do appreciate you taking care of Becky for me. She's the best thing Peter ever did."

After hanging up, she sat there on the floor, wondering what she was supposed to do now. If it were up to her, she'd hire someone to kill Peter off, then live a very happy life behind bars. But she'd made a promise to Rebecca that she'd not kill him or hire anyone to kill him. She'd feared for her life.

"Joey? Am I fired?" She looked up at Harvey and realized she had to be a nicer person. When a man older than her was afraid of her, then she was most certainly doing shit wrong. She told him she was sorry. "I knew you said no phone calls, but when he told me the police would be involved, I thought it best that he told you instead of the police showing up. That really would have upset you."

"It would have. You did the right thing in that." She told him again she was sorry. "I've been under a great deal of pressure with this work. I don't want to mess it up, and with all the stress of that, I tend to be snappish. I'll work on trying not to make you fear me in the future."

"I thank you for that."

She nodded, then stood up. When he went back to his desk, she went back to her workroom. Being a clothing designer wasn't as glamorous as people saw on television and in movies. It was difficult work trying to keep one step ahead of the people in the same industry. Not to mention having an idea what colors would be hot when the next season rolled around. Not that Joey put that much stock in the trends.

Joey designed for the everyday woman. No puffy sleeves for her. Nothing made of taffeta or silk for this line. She did design clothing for evening wear, but her meat and potatoes were the things that women wore every day to work or even for shopping — sturdy clothing that stood up well to time, washing, and the seasons.

"If you were to ask me if I'd wear that color, I'd have to tell you no. What is that called?" She looked over at her best friend and the woman that had given birth to her. Her mom was her partner too. Joey told her mom the color. "Pumpkin pie? You have got to be kidding me. If I had a pie of that color, I'd think it had turned. What are you going to mate it to?"

"Purple." When she picked up the paisley print she'd been searching for before the call came in, she hung it on the board in front of her next to the pumpkin pie. She knew it would work, but she still wanted her mom's opinion. "What do you think? Too much?"

"No. I think it works well. I can see this in a shirt and the pie in a pair of shorts, or even a nice pair of pants. I know you hate the word slacks, but that's what I was thinking of when I saw it. I really do like it." Nodding, she put the two colors on the plate with the design. "I have a feeling you're avoiding telling me about the phone call." Joey nodded but didn't look at her mom. "What is it, baby? Does it have to do with Rebecca?"

"She's gone." Mom nodded but didn't say anything as the two of them spoke quietly. "Becky is all right. Staying with a family in Ohio. I can't go there until they figure out what to do about Peter. I'm also not telling Margie."

"No. She'd be all over that. Crowing to the winds that she is going to be the next Mrs. Hightower. The two of them should have married, to begin with. Then it would have been over with for this family. You know as well as I do that she would have cut ties with us so quickly we'd need a birth certificate to prove she's related to us."

It was nearly nine that night when she heard from Becky. They talked for over an hour, and Joey felt so much better for it. She was being watched and taken care of. Also, she'd turned over the book and all the other things she'd collected in her young life to be put in the family safe. Joey wasn't sure how good of an idea that had been, but there was little she could do about it from here.

After hanging up with her niece, she was ready for bed. But a call from her sister, of all people, kept her up for the rest of the night.

"What happened today at work?" She asked Margie what she was talking about. "You. You got an important phone call that sent you to the floor. What is it? Rebecca again? If you know anything about her, you'd better be telling me, Joey. You know she's run off again with his child."

"How would I know she's run off? And the last time I remembered, Rebecca is a grown woman and can run off without people knowing about her whenever she wants. Are you having me spied on?" Margie said she was. "Why? What could you having me spied on do for you? I run a design shop, Margie. What on earth do you think you're going to find out by doing that?"

"You never know. I did find out you were upset, didn't I? Were you going to call me and tell me about it? Doubtful. When did you become so secretive, Joey? It's not a good look for you." Joey asked her sister when she'd become so paranoid that she had to have her watched. "When you started not taking my side when it came to Peter. He's a good man, you know. You should have more respect for him. All those things the paper is saying about him are lies, and you'd know that if you were to get to know him a little."

"I'm not even sure why you'd think I should care

what his life is like. As for what the papers say, your little spy should have told you I don't have a newspaper delivered, nor do I own a television." Margie told her she told her that. "Goodbye, Margie. I don't know where you got your information, but I'm not discussing my personal life with you. Call off your spy, or I will. And press charges."

It was a woman. Joey decided she was going to take measures she'd never thought she'd have to with her own family. Making two phone calls, she felt better for taking a stand. In the morning, only a few hours from now, she was going to do what she should have done long ago, start keeping an eye on those that worked for her. Joey had been slacking on a lot of things of late. Well, no more.

Chapter 1

Pierce looked over the file that he'd been handed just yesterday after sleeping for another five hours. It was about the Shepherd's store. As a part of the first time he went to a place that he'd been assigned, the health department would do an inspection as well as a complete background check into the people, and books were done separately from him. The reports usually got to him while still there. According to the letter accompanying the file, there were too many issues for it to have been submitted in a timely manner. Frowning, he opened the file while watching Demi wander around his office.

"For the record, I like that you do this. However, don't have them sent to me until you have gone over it. Some of that shit isn't anything I want to think about when I'm looking at what I might want for dinner. Yuck." Pierce laughed at Demi. "I kid you not, Pierce. Thinking of a watermelon exploding in a Gaylord box was too much. But to have pictures? Christ. Just sick. But tell me, what do you think the issues were that made the report come in so late?"

"The thing is, it happens a great deal with watermelon." He looked over the report. "They scored well. Clean bathrooms. Employees wash their hands. The only thing they got below a perfect score on is the parking lot cleanliness. I think the guy was looking very hard for something to be wrong, and that was what took so long. He was disappointed. There are a couple of things on my end. I'm not thrilled about the way they deal with the things that are out of date, nor what they end up doing with most of the food that is close to expiring. Couldn't you donate that to some kind of home before it's supposed to be going bad?"

"I honestly thought that was what they were doing. Not that it matters now, I suppose. I went there before this showed up. You're right about the lack of customers. Also, the markup on things was too much. Just as you pointed out." He told her what the management had told him about dynamic pricing. "Well, he priced himself right out of business. I did go by the other two places. You were right about them as well. Too close, and not even trying to compete with each other. I think a little healthy competition would benefit both."

Putting the file away, he watched her as she roamed around the room, sitting down only to hop up and over again. He was glad she'd come by, but he knew this was more than a follow up meeting. Pierce thought it was the baby she was carrying. She asked him what he knew about Hightower.

"Nothing more than what was in the paper recently. I have spoken to him on occasion when in the Shepard store. The man demands that people shop for him, then has the cart brought to him to approve of the things in it. However, he's being accused of a lot of things I have no doubt are true. Not that I believe his version of what happened to his wife, but as far as witnesses, there aren't any. His daughter is supposedly out there, as far as he knows. I no more think, even knowing she's safe, that her mom would have sold her to someone to hurt him than I think he's a nice man. He has been accused of doing most of the hurting. Why?" Demi didn't answer him right away. "Has the little girl or Meadow told you more since yesterday?"

"Both of them, as a matter of fact. One of them is that there is a book. I've seen it. I don't understand it, as it's written in some kind of code, but I'll get it." Pierce told her he had no doubt at all she'd get it. "I'm going to be a mom. I know you know that, but just the last few hours, I've been wondering what the hell I was thinking."

"You'll be a wonderful mom, Demi. I know you're worried about being like your mom was, or even your brother and sister. But I've seen you around the other kids in the family. You're great with them. And I also know my parents think you are going to be as well." He laughed a little. "I think Ian's daughters are picking up a few things from you."

She smiled at him. "Meadow is loving having Jilly work with her. I have to admit, it's fun seeing that little bit of a kid working a torch like she does. It's only the little stuff that she's doing, for now, clean up and such, but Meadow cannot believe how much she's getting finished by not having to do that." He asked her about Cybill. "Oh my, if there was more of a girly girl than that one, I don't know if I'd want to meet her. She is so frilly, don't you think?"

"She does have a style about her. But smart too. Both of them are." Demi told him how Jilly had tested out of all her high school classes and some college. "I heard that. But she doesn't want to celebrate it. I can understand that as well, not wanting to be the center of attention on things. I've always had a difficult time with that as well."

When she sat down again, he watched her face. It was nearly as unreadable as Meadow's. But the way her body stiffened on occasion made him think she was— Then it hit him.

"Are you in labor? Now?" She nodded at him. "Christ, woman. I'm not going to have to deliver your child, am I? Where is Lucian in all this?"

"He's on his way here to get me. I just needed some calmness before I went to the hospital. I knew you'd give it to me." He wasn't at all sure how to take that, so he just stood up. "Don't go all macho on me, Pierce. I need the fucking calm before the storm rolls in."

"Yes. All right." He tried his best to be calm looking. Inside he was a royal mess. Nodding and asking her if she needed anything, he nearly wet himself when she asked him if he could do a delivery. "Don't. Please, don't even joke about that shit."

"I was joking — sort of. I forgot to time them, so I've been doing that. They're about three minutes apart now." Pierce had no idea what that meant, so he screamed for Carol, his cook. After he told her what was going on, she sent him to find some blankets, as well as to boil water. It wasn't until he was in the kitchen with every pot he could find on the stove that he realized he'd been played. He turned off all the burners and went to the living room, where he expected to find them both laughing their asses off.

"Well? Are you going to just stand there or help me, you moron?"

Well, he should have known she'd be cursing up a storm while in labor. As soon as his brother arrived with their parents, Lucian carried Demi up to one of the bedrooms and laid her on the bed. Pierce stayed in his living room, not saying a word to anyone. Dad, however, was having the time of his life.

"I know I got me a whole bunch of grandbabies, some of them not so much a baby, but this is the first one born to the family. I'm a little bit excited about that. Have you called the others in?" He asked his dad if he should. "Don't know, to be honest. I would guess it might take a while. Don't know a thing about birthing with a human. Do you?"

"No. I guess I wasn't at school the day they talked about humans having a bear cub." Dad told him not to be a snarky, smart aleck. "She was in my home in labor, Dad. I think I have a right to be snarky, don't you? What if Lucian hadn't made it? What would I have done?"

"I don't know, son. Delivered the baby? You're a might upset about something we all knew was going to happen. What else has your panties in a twist? Is it closing down them stores?" Thinking about it for a second, he told his dad he really didn't know why he was so upset. "You do that a lot, son. You've got to be less stressful. Your momma told me you were going to be less stressed about stuff. Don't sound to me like that lasted all that long. I worry about you sometimes."

"I'm going to work on it. I think Demi just threw me off. She did say she came here for calmness. For some reason, that sort of hurt me a bit. I thought I was being too calm about things, but I think you're right—I'm stressing too much." He put his hand over his chest, right where his heart was. "I've been having some trouble lately with catching my breath when I get too worked up."

"Have you seen anyone about it?" He told his dad he'd been thinking it was nothing. "Well, I think you're thinking wrong. You go on out and get yourself an appointment. You might be a bear, but anyone dealing with stress is going to be a goner. Especially the way you've been going all your life. You need to just let it go."

"That might well be easier said than done." Dad told him to work on it, or he'd have him put in a hospital so someone would make him work on it." Nodding at his dad, they both stood up when Mom came down the stairs with a bundle in her arms. "She's finished?"

"What a thing to say. Yes, she's given birth. Just look at him. He's the spitting image of Lucian when he was a little one. Eleven pounder too." Before he could think about what he was saying, he said that sounded like a good sized turkey. "What is the matter with you? Did you just call your nephew a turkey? Pierce, I swear to John, there is something very wrong with you today. Do you need a snack or a nap?"

He didn't care for being treated this way in his own house, but he also knew better than to tell his mom that. She could and would take him to the woodshed on this. Not an actual woodshed, but he'd feel the sting of her anger at him all the way to his heart. Pierce told her he was sorry. Dad told her what he'd been telling him about stressing. Mom told Pierce to sit down and behave, then handed him the baby.

"He's so tiny."

Mom said he really wasn't, but he was too busy peeling the blanket from him to think about what she was telling Dad. When he unearthed his tiny hands, Pierce nearly sobbed out loud when the baby wrapped his little bitty fingers around one of his. His little fist wouldn't even fit around his finger.

Getting down on the floor with him, Pierce unwrapped him a little at a time. Discovering that he had all ten of his fingers, his toes were just as tiny as his hands. The fatty thighs nearly had him wanting to nibble on them. As he lay there, looking at the little guy, his brother joined him in the room.

"Why is my son on the floor?" Pierce just looked up at him. "He's a miracle, isn't he? I mean, I'd not say this to Demi, but doesn't he look like someone put a big person in the dryer for too long? Pierce, look at his toenails. They're no bigger than a pencil point."

"He took my hand into his. Well, my finger. I don't know why anyone wouldn't want to have fifty of these around all the time." The baby yawned, and both he and his brother, grown men, just about lost it. "Lucian, I want one of these."

"You have to find a mate first, moron. Are you still stressing?" Demi walked into the room. She didn't look like she'd just given birth to anything, much less the little guy he was looking at. "I told Cindy to bring him down here to you first. You did let us use your house. I'm sorry I freaked you out."

"I've been doing that a great deal lately." He wrapped him up again and handed him over to his brother. "Just the other day, I thought for sure I was having a stroke. I need to learn to chill out. I don't even know how to do that. But when I was resting at the house you lent me, I did a lot of thinking. I'm not sure what else I can do and make money. Understand?"

"You need to find your mate." He didn't bother saying anything back to Demi. That was something he thought they all strived for. "I'm serious here, Pierce. I'd just tell you to go and get laid, but you're not that sort of person. To have sex without some kind of attachment. I'm not saying you haven't, but—"

"Can we please change the subject? My parents are right there." Dad said he'd figured out a long time ago that his boys were having sex. "Christ, you guys need to gather your stuff up and go home. I have work to do."

"Nope. Everyone is coming here now to meet the baby. Why hasn't anyone asked his name?" He'd not even thought about it, he told her. "So you'd be all right if we were to just call him baby, or it, for the rest of his life?"

"Sure, why not? I mean, it would be easier than trying to remember it." She tossed a pillow at him. "What is his name, by the way?"

"Lucian Alden Morgan McCray." Dad sat down and pulled out his handkerchief. While he was wiping away the tears, Demi continued. "I have no one on my side to name him for, and that's why he's Alden. Grandma would have loved him called that."

"I do as well." Taking the baby from his mother, Pierce sat on the floor again with him. "I need a favor. From all of you. I need some help with my stress levels.

I've been having a great deal of trouble with…I guess you could call it holding it in. I can't continue to do that. Being on vacation showed me that I can't hold things in any longer."

"I wondered when you were going to ask for help." He looked at Demi. "It's not just the other day either, is it Pierce? Two weeks ago, I thought for sure you were going to die when you were in California for me. The manager you'd been sent to look into told me you had to sit down with your head between your knees for a good thirty minutes. Then there was just the other day when—"

"I know." He smiled at Demi. "I know. You'd think it would have scared some sense into me, but all it did was make me more determined to get things finished up. Like—I kid you not—I had to get things lined up for you before I died. Because you'd been so helpful to my family." When she stood up, Pierce asked her if she was going to hit him. "If so, please don't. It's taken me a while to get my head out of my ass and think of this the way you would. You didn't help us. You only gave us the tools to make things work for us."

"Pierce, I love you. Please, just learn to say I've got enough on my plate." He said he was going to work on that. "I surely hope so. Because if you keel over on me, I'm going to kick your ass until you wish you'd died."

"My goodness, Demi." Mom came and sat behind him in the chair he'd been in earlier. "Are you really that worried, Pierce? I know you well enough to know you're a person who likes things in order. Are you worried you might be taking on too much?"

"Not really taking on too much. However, I do—no. I did worry that if I didn't find things out that Demi and the others wanted to hear, they'd fire me. And I do love my job more than I can explain to you." Demi asked if he was giving her the truth of what he found. "Yes. Always. However, it is seldom good. I mean, I understand that is why you're sending me there, to find things that are going wrong. But it's always so wrong. I'm not making any sense, am I?"

"You are. And I know when I send you someplace, I'm not only going to get a good rundown of things, but you always include something you think will help it. Even if it's to tell me to shut a place down. As you did for Shepherd's." He said that was what was stressing him. "That I might have to shut a place down? Pierce, I'd rather shut a place down and lose a little money than keep one running to lose a great deal. You've done nothing but exactly what I wanted you to do. With the exception of making yourself sick. Please, for the love of it all, take a breather. I'm not ever going to shoot the messenger."

"I need to remember that too." He looked up at his mom while the baby slept on his lap. "I'm sorry I didn't tell you sooner."

"I'm just glad you've told me now. I want you to go see Doc Evans. He's more than likely going to tell you just what we've said, but I'd feel a good deal better if you'd see him. To make sure there isn't anything else wrong. Pierce, please, just be careful. I want all my sons to be healthy." He leaned back on her legs while he sat there. "Find you a mate and have you a houseful of little ones. That'll stress you out too, but it's the good kind."

"There is good stress?" They were all laughing when Demi took Alden up to the bedroom to rest. Lucian was going home to get some clothing for the two of them, then he wanted to spend the night. "I'd love that. I don't know what room you're in, but whichever it is, please make it your own. I'll never fill out these rooms at the rate I'm going."

Dad and Mom went home too. They were going to plan a nice celebration for the new baby and then come back later. Feeling a little better, Peirce didn't mind at all going to the store for Carol and getting some of the much needed foodstuffs it would take to feed his family. He was met at the door by Jilly.

~*~

"Aunt Mel has some things she needs to get done this morning. I could have stayed and cleaned up, but she said she'd rather I went out and had some fun. Since I knew you just got home, I wanted to spend some time with you. I'm glad you suggested having lunch."

"Me too. Mom was going to go and get some things for the baby, and Dad wants me to have fun too. I'm working on that." Demi had told them both to have fun. Jilly told Pierce she hadn't realized he was having issues. "Don't call them that. I'm stressing, that's all. I need to chill out."

"I don't know what you think issues are, but that is one." She looked around the restaurant, then back at him. "Ian told me you can read a person better than anyone he's ever met. I didn't have any idea what that might mean until I asked Aunt Mel. That's a cool thing to know how to do if you ask me."

"It is if you're looking at them in a positive way. That, I think, was my problem. I wanted to find the good in everyone." She told him she didn't think there were many people left like that. "I'm beginning to see that. Do you see that woman over there with the three kids? In about ten seconds, the kid with the frozen drink is going to dump it on her. On purpose too."

Right on time, the kid did just like Pierce said. The entire back of her skirt was covered in a sticky purple mess. Pierce went on to tell her that the woman wasn't their mom, more than likely not related to them at all. But she was dating their father, he thought. And she was trying to make a very good impression so she could be the next in line as their momma.

The woman simply walked away, leaving three kids there in front of the counter of the restaurant without anyone around them. She and Pierce watched as the kids started for the door. He told her they were going to hide so that when she returned, she'd be freaked out. Again, he was dead on with it.

"How do you know she's not their mother?" He asked her how the woman was dressed. "How she's dressed? Okay, I guess. Even Cybill wouldn't go to this place with a white skirt and a fur on. I bet you she'd be able to tell you what brand that was too. Cybill is weird like that."

"She's not weird, just not you." They both laughed as the woman pulled out her phone, crying, and made a call. The kids came back in the place and were seated at another table until a man came in, obviously pissed. "He's going to take it out on the woman if I don't miss my bet. She'll be happy to not have to be around the brats anymore. I blame that on him. They're terrible kids."

They watched the entire thing unfold. The man left without the woman. The kids didn't tell her they were sorry, and it was finished. Jilly looked at Pierce. She had wanted to talk to him for a few days now, but there hadn't been any time, it seemed. Today, she thought, was as good a time as any.

"There is this guy in one of my online classes that is pestering me." He didn't say anything, but then she knew Pierce well enough to know he'd get all the facts before he would tell her what to do. As soon as their dinner was set in front of them, she continued. "I've not told anyone. Lucy would have a fit. Ian would want to murder him, and I just want some advice on handling it on my own."

"What do you consider pestering? Since it's an online class, I'm assuming he's not doing anything to you personally." She told him not yet. "Not yet. So he's threatening you. With what, may I ask?"

"Okay. Now, this is going to sound way worse than it really is. He asked me for a picture of myself. I didn't send him one of me. I found a picture in a magazine and sent him that one. I don't want some pervert hanging my picture around so he can do his thing with it." Jilly felt her face heat up. "Anyway, he figured it out, and now he's threatening to tell everyone online that I'm ugly as sin—not that I care—but also that I've sent him naked pictures of myself. I swear to you, I didn't. Just that one picture, and that was it. I've tried ignoring him, but he's somehow gotten my email address. I've changed my password and even got a new email address when that didn't stop him. He's now sending me pictures. He's very naked."

"Why have you not told your sister or Ian?" She played with her napkin for a few minutes, trying to make her answer sound like she meant for it to. "You're afraid of them? Or what they might do to you?"

"No. I know they won't do anything to me. At least, I don't think so. But I don't think this guy is right in his head." She looked at her new uncle. "I was wondering if you could tell me if he's…I don't know. Off his noodle or something."

"The only person I know who can tell you that is

himself. Or Meadow. We can involve her, but she'll want you to tell Ian and your sister first." She thought that was what he'd say and said as much to him. "You knew that, yet you came to me first. I have a feeling there is more to this than just a kid sending you naked pictures. Give it up, Jilly. I can't help you if you don't tell me it all."

"He's the teacher of the class." She didn't look at him. Didn't look at anything other than her food. "I've been turning in all my homework, as well as the things he said we didn't have to do. That's how he was able to get into my email address, as well as the—"

"Meadow. I need you pronto."

When she suddenly appeared at the table with them, Jilly knew on some level that she wasn't really there. Pierce explained to her everything Jilly had told him, even asking her questions when he didn't know the answer. Meadow didn't say anything for several minutes, but she could almost feel her anger.

"I'm a little pissed that you let this go so far, Jilly. How long ago did he send you the picture of himself?" She said it was in her inbox that morning, but she'd not been checking it daily. "Okay. You have to tell Ian and Lucy. Mostly Ian, but Lucy will know because he'll tell her. This is bad—you know that, don't you?"

"Yes. I'm sorry." Meadow said she wasn't pissed off at her, only disappointed for her not coming clean sooner, but was furious with the man. "I've wanted to ask others in the class if he's done this, but I'm terrified he might have. Understand?"

"Yes. I really do. I'm sending Ian to you. He's in town with me right now. Honey, you will need to speak up about shit like this. He might well have been doing this a very long time, and no one spoke up. All right?" She nodded, then looked at her aunt. "What is it? You have more to share?"

"Yes. He's got my address too, I guess you know. Right now, there is a box in my room under the bed. That was there this morning too. I've not opened it. I don't plan on it, but I'm scared to death. That was why I ended up at Uncle Pierce's home when I found it. He's the closest to where we're living now. Please, don't be mad at me. I don't think I could take that."

Ian joined them, and Jilly had a feeling he'd already been briefed as to what was going on. Once he sat down, she confessed everything to him, including things she'd forgotten to mention to Meadow and Pierce. Like that, he was failing her for the class because she wasn't cooperating with him.

"I'll help him with his cooperation issues." She couldn't help it. Jilly laughed and cried at the same time. "Honey, I'm not pissed at you. Well, a little, but not nearly as much as I am at him. I'm going to take this fucker out, even if I have to step over dead bodies of my family to get to him."

Jilly shoved her food away, no longer wanting to put anything on her belly. As Ian worked with someone on the phone, she noticed other people in the restaurant coming and going. While she was watching the door, the teacher in question walked in and was seated in the room next to them.

"That's him?" Jilly told Ian it was that he must have followed her. "At least he's smart enough to know better than to sit next to you. The mother fucker. Lucy won't let me go near him until she and Meadow get here. I'd say he's in for a world of hurt. The police have gone by and gotten the package as well. I know you didn't want to cause any trouble, but this is much too important to a great many people for you to just try and work it out on your own. Next time, you have to let someone know."

"I will."

Her sister came into the restaurant and came to her. After giving her a hug, she told her she was grounded. "Not really. This isn't your fault. I'm upset with this fucker, but not at you. He's going to wish he'd never been born."

No one moved toward the table where the man was sitting. It made her sick to know he was watching her every move. Ian told her to act like she was having the time of her life, and Uncle Pierce told her a story about one of the people he'd observed one day. It was just what she needed to laugh. When his phone rang, Ian moved toward the door to take it.

Almost as if that was some sort of signal for them, the police came in the place with riot gear and guns out.

Meadow told her not to look in his direction but to talk to Pierce. She did, telling him how scared she was and that she'd never do that again.

"I know you won't, honey. I'm just glad you did come around to letting us know. Do you want to know what was in the box?" She nodded, then shook her head no. Then told him she did want to know. "Condoms. Used ones and new. Pictures of himself very naked, as you put it. As well as a note to you not to tell anyone or he'd have you expelled from school."

Going home later with Lucy and Ian, she felt so much better. It was like a giant ball of stress had been put on her, and she'd had no way of getting rid of it. When she was home, she went to Cybill's room and laid down. She needed time before she'd want to go into her room.

When she woke up, Cybill and her friend Becky were quietly reading on their readers. Sitting up, she told them she was sorry for being in their room. Cybill told her that Lucy had told them everything and that it was fine. She then asked what she was going to do about her room.

"I'm not sure. I mean, it's just the way I like it. And I didn't open the box in there. What would you do?" Cybill said she'd make it more frilly and put some bright colors in the room. "Okay, what do you think I should do? Keeping in mind that I'm not you."

"I'd leave it. Like you said, it's the way you want it, and he's never been there." Cybill looked at her. "I'm sorry this happened to you, Jilly. I'm glad you finally told someone, but I'm really sorry that someone soured things for you for a while."

"I'll be all right." She thought about being expelled. "I don't think he can do that. At least that was what I was told. I'm going to take a break for a couple of weeks, then get back to it. He did sour things for me a little."

After going down to the living room, she was happy to see things were going along as normal. They were going to a party later, she was told, to welcome the newest McCray baby. She was looking forward to that. Mel had helped her order the baby a gift online, and it had been wrapped and ready to go for a couple of weeks now. Feeling better all the time, she was glad she'd gone to Pierce first. He'd paved the way so that Lucy didn't freak out on her. And she did sometimes.

Chapter 2

Joey hated to wait on things to progress. She wasn't so much impatient as she was ready to do battle. When the call had come to her the other day about her sister-in-law, she wanted to drop everything and go rescue Becky. But that would only cause the little girl more trouble than she could help her out with.

"Have you figured it out yet?" Looking at her mom, she just shook her head. "Is this room the only one you have debugged daily? I'd do it more often, but this is a good start. I'm so sick of Margie that I want to hunt her down and shake her hard. Or snap her neck."

"My goodness, Mother. Such violence nowadays." The two of them laughed. "I think the part I hate most about this is that I've had to shut all my blinds in here. I haven't any idea if she has someone reading lips or not, but I'm going to try my best to keep her in the dark for as long as I can. Did I tell you she called me last night? Why on earth she can't call to bitch at me at a decent time is beyond me. But it was four in the morning."

"I did as you asked me to do and called Harvey at home. He's terrified of losing his job. But he did tell me he'd call you every time Margie came to him for information. He's also started putting all his files on a thumb drive and taking it home with him every night. That was an excellent idea you had." Nodding, she told her mom that Harvey had been investigated now, and she trusted him. "I don't know that I'd trust anyone anymore. To think that we have spies working right here with us."

"I have something to tell you. I've been waiting for the right time, so just don't freak out." Mom told her it wasn't in her nature to freak out. "This might take you over the edge. The people that have Becky have this magic around them. A great deal of it from what I'm to understand. One of them, I don't remember her name, can be out on a walk with Becky right beside her, and Peter wouldn't see either of them. They're that good and taking care that no one can see her."

"Okay, that is a little freaky. How is this going to help you get there?" She said she had to wait on this man to come here to ferret out who her spy was. "That's necessary to have done before you leave?"

"Meadow, that's her name. She told me that leaving the spy here would only open myself up for all kinds of shit to go on here. Like having orders sabotaged, computers cloned, and other things that would kill our business. You know as well as I do that we're only just making a name for ourselves. If it was to be hurt now, it'd be years, if ever, before we get it back to where we are now." Mom nodded and asked when the man was coming. "Today sometime. He's going to be working with me in the design room. That is the most centralized place he can see people. His name is Pierce, brother or something to Meadow."

"So he's some kind of profiler then? Do you know either of their last names? Anything at all about where they're coming from?" Joey told her mom she supposed that would be as good a name as any. "Then what happens after he finds them? Do you just fire them? This seems a bit more dangerous than I would have thought. Don't you think?"

"It's less dangerous than me running to wherever she is and getting myself and Becky killed. Margie is calling in all kinds of favors to figure out where she is. Meadow has her finger on a great many things that she knows Margie is doing. Like the bugs in my office. Yesterday I thought they were all gone, and suddenly this woman appears in front of me. She shows me where one is that was missed." Mom didn't say anything but did lean back in the seat she was in. "My house is bugged too, did I tell you? I'm not staying there right now, so if you need me, I'm here. Your home is going to be taken care of today if you don't mind."

"Why?" Joey asked her mom what she meant. "Why would he go to all this trouble for one little girl? I can understand wanting her back — I really do — but she's not bothering him right now. And we know his wife is dead. He might not know it yet, but I'm betting he's figuring on that. Why is all this cloak and dagger stuff going on for a small child that never meant a thing to him?"

It took Joey a moment to answer her mom. She trusted her with her life. But it seemed to her lately that she was asking all kinds of questions. It worried her on so many levels that she really couldn't trust anyone but herself and Pierce, as Meadow had told her. Instead of fobbing her off, she decided to tell her the truth. For now.

"She has his book." Mom didn't understand, so she explained. "Where he's planted bodies, I guess. Who owes him favors. Who he can count on to get laws passed that he wants in his favor."

Mom did look freaked out then. "I thought that was just a myth, that bad guys did that sort of thing." She told her mom what Meadow had told her. "So they need to break the code. And this woman, she thinks she can get into his house and find it? Christ, that's scary, Joey. Your sister wants this man in her life? Is she insane?"

"Yes. I'd say so. She was never like you and I. Since the first time she found out about men, sex, and money, she's been after the next biggest thing." The door to her office was locked all the time now, so when it was rattled, like someone was coming in, she waited. "I'm betting it's Margie. You wait and see what she has to say to me about all this shit I have going on."

Getting up, she moved the blind to see that it was indeed her sister. After Joey asked her what she wanted, not opening the door, Margie banged her fist on the door. Opening it up, Joey moved back before she was able to hit her. That seemed to piss Margie off even more.

"What the hell do you think you're doing?" Joey went to sit with her mom, finishing up her lunch that she didn't really want. "You're having too much fun out of what I have going on around here, Joey. You're not playing fairly with what I need from you."

"And what do you think I have that you want?" She asked her where Becky was. "With her mother, I would guess. I have no idea. If I did, do you think I'd be here and not with her? Go home, Margie. I told you when I spoke to you the other day that I was going to get your spies out of here. This is just one more layer of precaution I'm taking."

"Not that it matters much. I'll soon know what you know." She looked at Mom. "Still not dead yet, are you Mother dear? You should have let me marry Peter when I was younger. None of this would be necessary if you had."

"You were only sixteen, Margie. I wasn't going to let a child marry anyone. No matter how rich he was." Margie huffed at her. "As it was, he married his wife when he should have been looking for women his own age. The poor woman was raped until she got pregnant with his child."

"He wouldn't have had to rape me." Mom just turned away from Margie. "I want you to take down these ridiculous blinds and stop having the room gone over. It's not like you're telling any kind of state secrets, Joey. Just go along the way you were, and you won't have to get hurt."

"I would ask you if you just threatened me, but I know you'd just smirk at me. I'm doing this because, while I'm not telling state secrets, the very thought of you knowing what I'm doing in my own place of business is pissing me off." Margie picked up Joey's salad and threw it against the wall. "Very mature. If you think that is going to bring out some sort of temper in me, think again. You've been a bully all my life. I'm over you."

"Will you be over me if this place were to suddenly burn to the ground? Would you come back to me, crawling on your hands and knees, begging me to leave you alone? Even if you did do that, I'd never let you have a moment's peace. I want to know where Becky is. She's stolen something from her dad, and he wants it back." She asked her what it was. "None of your business."

"Oh, so you can know all my business, but I'm not allowed to know yours." Margie said that was right. "Tough shit, Margie. I'm not now, nor will I be in the future, afraid of you. In fact, I'd say you should be watching your own back from now on. As soon as I get the spies caught, I'm going to have you arrested. You being here, with me having a court-ordered restraining order against you, is enough to get you put in jail. Go home before I make good on calling the police."

Margie picked up Mom's salad and looked like she was going to throw it as well. But Mom took it back from her and set it on the table. Eating it with gusto, she smiled at Margie. She did wonder where her mom got her gutsy ways sometimes.

After she left, Joey sat with her head laying on the table. Just as she was sitting up to tell her mom she'd had enough, a man knocked on the open door and smiled at her. Christ, he was the best looking man she'd seen in about—well, all her life. He said his name was Pierce.

While she knew the man's last name, she didn't mention it. Joey also knew to call him Sander. It was supposed to be his middle name or something. The notes she'd taken while talking to Meadow were in her hotel room where she'd left them. Things, she knew, were going wrong here on so many levels she wasn't sure which end was up anymore.

"Hello." He nodded at her mom but didn't take his eyes off her. "You're supposed to be someone that can profile the people that work here? Must be a boring job. Watching people all day to see if they make any mistakes and give themselves away."

"On the contrary, it's very much fun for me. I can tell a great deal about a person when they think they're hiding something. Like you, for instance." Joey tensed up, knowing he was going to tell her that her mom was part of the spy ring. "You've been hurt recently. Mostly in your ribs, so your daughter here wouldn't notice. I'm sure she has, but it's not occurred to her that you'd keep something like that from her. Also, your car has been hit in the last twenty-four hours. That I know because there was a police report done on it. I'm not that good."

"Mom? Is he telling the truth?" Mom nodded, then burst into tears. Pierce simply moved to the door and closed it on his way out. "Why didn't you tell me? Was it Margie? One of Peter's goons?"

"I was coming out of my house when I felt something hit me. I figured out later it was some kind of drug that was in a dart. The little thing is still in the house but in a safe. When I woke up, I was hurting so badly I couldn't breathe. Then I got this call from some man telling me that if I didn't cooperate, I'd not be out the next time. I'd feel it all." She asked her mom what they wanted. "The same thing. Information. I don't want you to tell me anything more, Joey. I'm afraid of what they'll do to me if I don't tell them whatever it is you tell me. I'm an old woman who can't handle too much in the way of pain anymore."

"You're going on vacation." Mom told her she'd be all right. "Perhaps, but I'm not going to take any chances with you. Before you leave here today, everything will be set up for you. Don't tell anyone. I'll stop your mail and figure out your plants and such. You don't even pack,

Mom. It's a spree for you. All right?"

"Yes. All right."

Mom was still crying when she asked Pierce to come back into her office. He had been sitting at one of the empty desks just looking on the computer. But she had a feeling that not only could he tell her what was going on with each person there, but that he might well have a good idea who the spies were. He came into her office and sat down by her mom.

"She has to get out of here." Pierce told her it had been arranged by one of his sisters. "Just like that? You're going to get my mom out of here even though you don't know if she's one of the spies?"

"Your mom might well have been convinced to spy on you had we not come here today. She's been hurt and threatened with something that very few know about her." He looked at her mom intensely. "You have to tell her what you know, Lauren. If it comes out that you knew this, there isn't any saving you when this shit hits the fan."

Mom nodded and Joey sat back down. Not because she wanted to be near her mom, but because her knees simply would not hold her any longer. This was too much. It was overwhelming her that all this was happening. Asking her mom what was going on, she knew this was going to be just about as bad as it could be.

"About five years ago I had an affair. It wasn't like it was an affair, I suppose. I've been a widow longer than

I was a wife. But it was fun. A fling, I guess you could say. However, I hadn't any idea Peter was having things recorded between us. Not only was he recording it, but other things were done that I wasn't aware of." That didn't sound so bad, but her mother looked at her in the eye. "He has a video of us. I don't have any idea how it happened — as I said, it was just a fling — but he and I are in bed with several other people. Men and women. It's horrid, Joey. Just terrible. I paid this other man off with most of my money, then borrowed the rest from you. I thought I had the only copy. It seems now that it's starting to come out again. I just don't know what to do about it."

"When you asked to get your house in order." She nodded. "This man, this person, he's blackmailing you now, I take it."

"Not Blake, but someone who says they have a copy of it. I'm sure Peter is behind it all. If I don't tell his man everything we discuss, he'll put the video out there, and it will ruin all this for you too." Joey shook her head. "Yes, it will, Joey. As you said earlier, we're just starting to make a name for ourselves, and this will ruin it all."

"We only just found out about it yesterday. I wasn't supposed to start until after you and I sat down to talk." Pierce told her how sorry he was as he continued. "My sisters-in-law are finding out who has the original. They don't think Blake has it. From what we've found out, he's being blackmailed too. Demi thinks he is as unaware of how the video came about as your mom is."

"Blake Daniels." He nodded. "So, my mom had an affair with this man who is as single as she is, and someone either doctors it up to make it look sordid, or they did something to make my mom and Blake unaware of what was happening. Can your family figure that out?"

"Meadow, whom you've spoken to, said it's not doctored, but she also knows it isn't your mom or Blake. They're body doubles. That's all we've been able to figure out so far." She told Pierce that was more than she had at the moment. "Yes. There is more, but it's nothing like this. We'll get it figured out, and once they do, there will be a reckoning they'll feel for a very long time."

"I don't understand why your family would go to all this trouble for me. And my mom, of course. What gives here?" Pierce took his time answering, so much so that she cut him off when he opened his mouth. "This has more to do than with just Becky coming to your home. Doesn't it?"

"It does, but now isn't the time to discuss this. The people are here for your mom, and we need to get her out of town. There won't be any contact between the two of you for a while. But she'll be watched as if it's you watching her." Joey told Pierce she didn't know why she should trust them. "Because you need help, and we're the only people at this point that can help you. I'm not saying they won't get their jail time, but with the magic and powers we hold, no one is going to come out of this on the upper end of the food chain unless we say they can. That would include your mom."

"And she'll be safe? Nothing will happen to her?" He said the way they had it fixed, nothing would happen unless her mom decided to do things her own way. Joey looked at her mom. "You'll do what they tell you. Do you hear me, Mom? I don't want you hurt or killed. If they tell you to jump off a ship, then you ask them how far out. Okay? I can't lose you."

"I'll promise you I'll do everything they tell me." Mom stood up. Giving her a much needed hug, Mom looked at her. "You take care as well, my darling. After I'm gone, Margie is going to double her efforts in hurting you."

Two women came into the room with them and shut and locked the door. Taking Mom to her bathroom, they worked with Mom while Joey waited with Pierce. Neither of them said anything, but he did make notes on a small notepad. It was all she could do not to snatch it from him and tear it to pieces.

"You're very tense." She laughed, but it was horrible sounding even to her. "I'd say to close up and not reopen for a while, but I know that's not a possibility right now. I've been reading up on what you do here. Even though it's only a few weeks from Christmas, you're getting your summery wardrobe out. My niece, Cybill, handed me some notes on my way out this morning. She's one of your biggest fans. Her sister calls her a girly girl."

"Into fashion, is she? I don't cater to the rich and stupid much. That wasn't nice, I know, but I don't do skinny models or clothing that a housewife would never imagine herself wearing. I'm more of a person that makes things for the average person, who either works outside the home and has a busy life or might work from home but still wants to feel pretty." She got up and picked up the folder she'd been working on all morning. "This is what I was doing for summer this year. I haven't any idea if anyone will think these colors are the go to colors, but I like them. That's another thing I do—I do what I want. So far, it's worked out very well for us."

"Cybill said you usually pick colors from the color chart that no one has ever seen before. I'm taking notes here on some of the colors I've seen here. As for her being into fashion, she is, very much so. Her sister is not only not into fashion, but just the other day, I had to get a few of my sweatshirts from her that she'd taken because where she works is cold. They're way too big for her, as you can imagine."

"How old is the sister?" Pierce told her. "She's not cold, Pierce, but hiding the fact that she might be big chested or something along those lines. I'm betting her sister shows off her body in everything she wears."

"She does." The door to the bathroom opened up, and there stood three people. If she had to say one of them was her mom, she'd be hard pressed to know which one it was. Standing up when Pierce did, he introduced her to the two women. "This is Demi. Meadow is the other woman there. Between the two of them is your mom. What do you see?"

"You. You're there between them." Joey looked at him, then back at her mom. "How the hell did you pull this off? Mom? Is that really you?"

"Yes. Oh my, it's working." They explained to her what was going on. Her mother hadn't changed, but Meadow had made her mind see Pierce, not her mom. "They said the three of us will walk out of here. Everyone here will think Pierce is gone for the day. But I'll be safe enough to leave here without any trouble."

After the three of them left, Pierce stayed in her office for the rest of the day. She was too upset with everything to do much more than stare at her boards. Finally giving up, she made her way to her office and sat down at the computer. Pierce was working on his laptop. She was able to ignore him for the rest of the day and well into the evening. Getting work done had never been so stressful for her.

~*~

Pierce stretched out on the little couch and wished for the hundredth time that he'd thought to bring a sleeping bag. Not that he'd have been able to slip it into the office without raising awareness of it, but he would have liked to have had more than the little piece of material he'd been using since Joey left.

His mate. He'd known she would be when he'd been asked to come here. Not that he was going to tell her yet. She had enough going on that telling her that might make her head explode. Several times during the day, he'd reached into her mind to calm her, and each time he was hit with such a jumble of thoughts and fears that he finally just gave up. Mel spoke to him just as he was getting ready to give up on sleeping.

There are three things you need to know before tomorrow morning. Harvey, her secretary, isn't playing ball with Margie. He has too much respect for Joey and her mom to turn on them. So I've taken it upon myself to give him a little more protection while he's not at work. He's really a nice man. Pierce told her that was good. *I've also put in an order for you to have some things sent to you. They'll arrive sometime during the lunch hour. The entire staff will be gone, and that'll be the perfect time for you to get them set up.*

I didn't notice that everyone leaves for lunch here. Some do. What did you do to make it so they're all gone? She said Meadow made it so they were to get a free lunch at the restaurant across the street. *I suppose that will work. What else? You said three things.*

Third thing is, and I probably should have started with this, her mom is safe. I've put her in one of the houses here so she can get some much needed help with her injuries. I thought about putting her on that cruise they spoke about, but I couldn't be as diligent in keeping an eye on her if I did that. Also, in addition to that, I've taken care that Blake is safe. The man is being hurt by this as well. She went on to tell Pierce about the house she had for him to use instead of a hotel room. Mel said he could use either, but she would prefer that he used the house.

I would imagine there are too many people going in and out of there too. What about Joey? That was who he was most concerned about, and Mel had guessed why.

She's your mate, isn't she? Pierce told her she was, but not to tell anyone, or they'd all be there with him. *I thought that was your reasoning. I like her so far. She's cooperating big time, and that is going to end this sooner rather than later. Also, you can show her the pictures I'm sending to your phone. They're of Becky. It'll help her to know she's safe.*

That's a wonderful idea. There are a couple of people here I'd like for you to look into for me. I'm not saying they're in on it, but they've had a huge influx of cash put into their accounts. It was easy enough to break into them since they all have direct deposits for their checks here. He gave her both names. *Carole Rankin said she got a windfall from her mother's estate. I looked — her mother did pass, but I don't see where she had enough for her to be spending, mostly paying off big debts, the way she is. But I have been known to be wrong once in a while. Could be just some insurance. The other, Wanda Smith, just seems weird to me. Could be she's just out there, but something about her makes even my bear want to hurt her.*

I'll have you something in a little while. Anyone else I can look into for you? Oh, speaking of which, the name Janice Pike. Is she an employee there? Pierce pulled up the staff's records and told her she'd been terminated some time ago—five years. *She's still getting a check. See what you can find out about that from Joey. Could be nothing more than her not being taken off the payroll. But to be honest with you, Pierce, I'd think Joey would have noticed a check going out for someone that doesn't work there.*

According to this, the checks are okayed by Joey's mother. It looks like each check going out is signed by her. Do you think she's taking the money for herself? Mel told him she didn't have any idea. *I'll put that on my list of things to talk to her about. The room is debugged daily here, and the blinds are closed against anyone seeing what she's doing in Joey's office. I don't know why, but I'm thinking we're missing something here. Whatever it is, I can't seem to locate it. I've been all over this room several times.*

Which reminds me. Some of the equipment you have coming in is going to help her with debugging her office. It won't find them, but it will render them unworkable. Just set the device on her desk, and nothing within a five-mile radius will work. He asked her why so far. *The parking garage next door is where the employees park. I didn't want them going out and using whatever they need out there. Plus, I'm betting they talk shit in the garage. I believe this will render their car bugs unusable as well. But that only works for as long as they're within the five miles.*

After she told him what else he was going to be getting, including the company credit card he'd forgotten, the connection was closed. He wandered around the floor then, looking for things out of the ordinary or even things that would give him a better outlook on the people he was there to check out. Three of them had to go — he'd known that even before coming here. The hard part would be convincing Joey that what he found out about them was worth firing them over.

He'd been planning to have donuts brought in, but since he wanted them all out of the office at lunchtime, he didn't want them to be too full and not want to go. When Joey came in about six-thirty, he'd already written out some notes for her to go over with him. He'd also made himself a nice pot of tea. Pierce noticed that she mostly only drank water, which was good for her.

"Are we clean in here?" He shook his head, and they went to the board where she had all kinds of different fabrics hanging. "I got an email from your niece last night. I guess you sent her some pictures of the colors I'm using. She told me that she aspires to being like me someday. Creating clothing that just anyone can pull off."

"She thinks her sister is a slob just so you know." They both laughed about that, and he handed her a note that had nothing to do with what he was telling her verbally. "These are the colors she suggested. I hope you don't mind, but I've had a look at them, and they do seem to have a little bit to do with everything here."

Joey seemed to understand and wrote on the paper, "Fire them?" At his nod, she nodded as well. He could do it for her. In fact, he'd enjoy helping her out with this sort of thing. When he handed her the second note, this one about the lunchtime bug out, she only put it in her front pocket and nodded again. He could tell she was upset with all this. Pierce knew he would be as well. Firing people wasn't fun. But neither was having people spying on you all the time.

"While we're talking here, can you tell me what this is about?" She took the note he'd made with the name of the person checks were being written to by her mom. "We can talk about it later if you wish."

"No. It's fine. Janice worked for me when I first started out. She was amazing. But she was killed one night after leaving here. I've been helping her family out since then. I know that I'm not responsible for her family, but she was one of the kindest people I knew." Pierce told her she was very kind in helping them. "I wish I could do more. Mom and I decided her young children could use a little extra since their mom is gone."

Chapter 3

Joey couldn't concentrate on anything. Her mind bounced between her job and her mom to the man that seemed to be right there all the time. Not in an intrusive way. He was never underfoot. He didn't speak until she asked him something. And when she did ask him, he had a good solid answer that would make her feel like he'd been paying attention to her babbling. Looking out over the people that worked for her, she stared at the two empty seats that had been used by two people she thought she could trust. Harvey came toward her with a few sheets of paper, and when she dodged him, just a little, Pierce took it from him. Harvey didn't seem to mind and spoke to Pierce about whatever was written on them.

That was another thing. He seemed to know enough about what she was doing that he could even answer calls from buyers and suppliers. She knew that twice he'd had to go and find someone to help him. Asking for help was something she encouraged everyone to do. Joey hadn't had to say a single word to him about it either.

"I'm having some trouble getting on the Internet." Her first thought was that it was the device on her desk. She wasn't too terribly comfortable about it being there and cutting off things. "We're not allowed to surf the Internet anymore? I do my work, you know."

Debby, she thought her name was, was on Pierce's list of potential termination candidates. According to the records he pulled up, she spent about sixty-six percent of her time on the Internet playing games and reading about the royals. Twenty more percent answering her emails from her personal account. That wasn't getting her work done as far as Joey was concerned.

"We throttled down on the usage of the Internet while on the job. If you're having trouble, it might be because it's one of the sites that isn't on the approval list I handed out this morning." She said she always checked her email from her computer. Sent things out too. "I'm sorry it's messing up for you. But I did explain that, since we're cutting back on staffing, we'd all have to work more efficiently."

"I don't care for this. I'm just putting that out there because you said it would be all right if we came to you with a beef. Changing the rules in the middle of the week isn't very nice." She pointed out that she'd been told about that company policy when she was hired. "Everyone does it. Why are you singling me out?"

"I'm not. I'm singling out everyone, especially

those that don't cooperate with me on this." She didn't break eye contact with the woman but watched as she started away. When she turned and asked where her mom was, she had the answer ready to go. The McCray family had thought of everything. Or so it seemed. "She's taking some time off. Apparently, she was hurt a few nights ago and isn't healing the way she had hoped. If you want to send her a get-well card, I'll make sure she gets it."

"Since I can't email her on company time, then I guess she won't know I care that she's gone."

Turning her back on the girl, Joey made a mental note to get her ducks in a row about firing her as well. She didn't need someone harping on things she'd been doing wrong all along and was only now being told no more.

"Here you go." She took the tall glass of iced tea from Pierce and sipped it. It was so good; however, she drank it almost straight down. When he winked at her, she laughed. He was like a breath of fresh air today. "There are three things I need to tell you. One of which you may or may not be aware of."

The note he handed her while he spoke never had anything to do with what he was telling her. It was, she thought, working out very well for the two of them— until now. Looking at the note two more times, she looked up at him.

"Is this right?" He nodded and sat down on the

corner of the desk he'd been using. "I see. I guess I should have guessed."

"No reason for you to have known. It's not something I tell a great many people. It will only take a nip." He wanted a taste of her blood so he could communicate with her while they were working. She was afraid someone would get ahold of the notes they were passing back and forth now that she thought about it. "I have some things in your office to make that work if you'd like."

"Yes. I think that might be a better route than this." She handed him back the note, and the two of them went into her office. Almost as soon as the door closed behind him, the phone on her desk started ringing. "It's more than likely a buyer."

"Nope. It's your sister. She calls every time you or both of us come in here. Let me nip your flesh. It won't hurt." She nodded and put out her hand for him. "I should have told you this the other day when I met you. I won't do this without you knowing what it means between the two of us. I'm your mate. I know you understand that, as you have shifters working for you. I'm a bear, black in the event you wish to know. All of my family are, for the most part. Mostly more than that, but when you meet them, you'll get it."

"Are you sure...? Never mind. I know you are. There are things I should have picked up on, but I've been too busy trying to get my shit together. What happens if you bite me? Or if I bite you?" He told her. "That doesn't seem so bad. I mean, being able to find me is a good thing—especially in light of all this other shit. Also, I don't know why, but you have calmed me when I need it. Like…I suppose you can feel my needs and can act on them before I explode."

"I don't know that you'd explode per se, but I can feel them. Mostly because I've been keeping an eye on you. But yes, I'd have a better hold on your emotions so I can help you when you need it." She nodded. "You decide if this is what you want, Joey. I'm not going to force you into anything. Ever. I want you to be comfortable enough to trust me when you need me."

"I haven't any idea why, but I already do." She looked around her office, then at him. "I'm afraid if you want the truth, not of you, but of all this and what it will do to me. I love what I do, and I'm having a good time. But in the back of my head, all I can think about is that my own flesh and blood is out to get me. Do you think they're going to kill me if they don't get what they want?"

"How about we talk about that later? If it comes up." She thanked him. "No need for that, Joey. As I said, I want you to be in the know of everything going on, and this will make it easier for the two of us to talk. Because of the connection you'll have with me, if you wish it, you'll be able to talk to the rest of my family as well. They're rooting for you to come out ahead. I believe with all I am that you will."

Nodding, she put out her hand for him. The lick to her palm was sort of breathtaking. The bite, no more than a small prick of her skin, didn't even make her flinch. When he offered up his hand, he used a pin he had in his hand to cut into his skin. The sight of his blood bubbling up on his hand had her licking her lips. His low growl made her look at him.

"You're a very beautiful, desirable woman, Joey. Just take my blood before I toss you onto your desk and show you how much I'd like you naked beneath me." She smiled at him, looked at her desk, then licked his hand. Picking up the phone, she answered it, knowing it was Margie.

"What the hell do you want now? Don't you think I have more important things to do than to listen to you harp and harp about what you think I should be doing for you? Don't call here again, or so help me, Margie, I'm going to have you arrested for harassment." Slamming the phone back down on the cradle, she turned to him. "Was that really her, or did I just piss off some potential buyer with that call?"

"It was her. Meadow has someone watching her all the time. Just after it rang, she told me it was your sister. Meadow said she'd give you a heads up on her calls if you wish." She said she would. *All right. When people speak to you through this link, you might have some trouble figuring out who they are. All voices, until you understand things about them, are basically the same. Neutral. So don't be afraid to ask who it is. Do you have any questions about how I'm speaking to you?*

No. She grinned at him. *So all I need to do is just think of you and talk. I like that. How do I put the word out that I need your entire family to listen up? I mean, I'm sure you have that figured out as well.*

You just need to think of needing help, and that will put out a call to all of them. She nodded and opened the door to the office but turned back to him when he said her name in her mind. *I wasn't kidding when I said I'd like to take you on your desk. I'm not having any trouble keeping my hands off you right now because you're stressed out, and we only want to help you. However, when this is over, Joey, I'm not sure how long I can wait to have you.*

I want you too. But not yet. I'm not teasing you. I'm really not, but I think I'm just too stressed to deal with one more thing. Not that you're a bad thing, don't take it like that, but I have a murdering man and my sister out there somewhere trying to get me to do something I know is against the law. Not to mention, they killed a very nice person for no other reason than they could. She moved back into the room then, letting the door close behind her. *This will have to do for now.*

Joey only meant for it to be a short kiss to his mouth. But almost as soon as her lips touched his, she wanted much more than just his mouth touching hers. However, the knock at her door prevented her from taking as much as she could. Pierce held her away from his body while he spoke to Harvey on the other side. Joey was way over her head with this man, she thought.

"The staff just won the free lunch I was telling you about. They're wondering if you'd allow them to go out just a little early to get in line. There isn't going to be a line. The restaurant doing this is only serving your people today. But sending them out will give us enough time to get things finished up here." She asked him what things. "The equipment that is downstairs in the lobby now. I can have it set up in no time, but this way, we won't have to be rushed."

Going into the main room of her business, Harvey handed her a copy of the email.

"It says here it's all expenses paid. That's wonderful." She smiled at the people in the room. Some of them already had their coats on, ready to go. "I tell you what. Since this is a special treat for you guys, why don't you take a two hour lunch? I'm not getting much done here anyway, so that might be just enough time for me to drink a nice hot cup of cocoa and get my act together."

They were all gone except Harvey in less than five minutes. He handed Pierce a file and left too. The silence of the room had her closing her eyes and relishing in the first bit of quiet she'd had in some time. Pierce went to the hallway and took the elevator to get what she could only assume was the equipment. She was glad now that the debugger had come earlier. The peace of mind it was giving her had helped a good deal already.

Not only did Pierce get all the equipment set up

with plenty of time left over, but the cameras were all around the room over each desk in a way that not only could she see their computer screens, but also anything laying on their desks. Joey didn't care for doing things this way, but this was, she thought, a matter of life and death. Perhaps not hers, but Becky and her mom's.

When the employees came back, she thought they all looked as if they had enjoyed their lunch. The only person complaining was Debby, and that was because they wouldn't allow her to have a free glass of wine with her meal. Filing that away with her other notes on the girl, she did point out they were still on the clock, and perhaps they'd done the right thing. Of course, Debby didn't agree. Free should have meant all of it was free.

"You drank a glass of wine on my company time? You know you can be fired for that, don't you?" Two of the people near her desk said she'd actually had four glasses. "I think it's time you left here, Debby. I can't have you drinking on your lunch hour then coming back here to work. I have to think about what this means for you and my company."

"You're joking, right?" Joey told her she wasn't. "I'm not intoxicated. Perhaps if you got laid once in a while or even had a glass or two yourself, you'd not be such a bitch about every little thing. Why the hell won't you give him what he wants? Christ, it would be better for all of us, being on pins and needles all the time, if we didn't have to worry about some jerk jumping out wanting information on you. It is his kid."

Pierce was right behind Joey when she started backward. Whether she was falling or moving, she didn't know, but he told her the police were on their way. Debby apparently had more to say and was telling anyone who would listen to her how Joey had taken a kid and was hiding her away from her own father. She even mentioned he'd find her mom too.

Joey was so shook up by the time the police arrived that she let Pierce handle the entire thing. As she was sitting in her office, wondering where the hell she'd fucked up so badly that this was happening to her, someone tugged at her mind. At least that was what it felt like.

This is Cindy, honey. I'm Pierce's mom. She told her she couldn't speak right now. *I know, honey. Mel and Meadow are here with me, and they've told me what is going on. I'm so sorry, dear. I really am. But I want you to think about coming here for the weekend. It's only Wednesday, but you think on it. No one will know you're here, and you can see your mom and Becky too. I've only just been told that you and Pierce are mates. I'm so happy for you both.*

He's been like a rock for me. Making no demands. But it's like he knows what I need even before I do. She told her that was what mates did for people. *You said no one would know I'm there. Are you sure about that? I don't want to cause any of you any trouble—especially not my niece and mother.*

They'll never know. You have my word on it. Joey

thought she'd enjoy being around nice people for a change. *Good. I'm going to let the girls here make the arrangements, and then they'll get back to you. Welcome to the family, Joey. I think you're going to fit right in with the rest of us.*

After they finished making arrangements, she decided this was going to be good for her. While she hadn't any idea what sort of background Peirce came from, she had an idea he was from a good home. How on earth could they raise a son like Pierce and not be a good family was her way of thinking.

Debby was taken away, and Pierce came into her office. When he left the door open, she figured he'd put the fear of her into them if they came into the office. Instead, he sat down on the couch and smiled at her when she asked him what was going on.

"I've sent everyone home." She nodded, not even caring that she was going to be even more behind. "The officer wants them to each fill out a sheet of paper telling him what went down at the restaurant, then here. I figured you'd not be getting anything done anyway, so I just took it upon myself to let them go."

"Your mom invited me to come to her home for this weekend. I'm not entirely sure what that means, but I'm going. Even if you don't." He laughed. "I'm assuming you and your family has money. The names on some of the equipment show it is some high end stuff. Also, that there is more than just you and your two sisters-in-law."

"There are. In addition to my parents, there are six

of us sons, counting me. Four of them are married. That does not include you since I've not asked yet to marry you. Nieces and nephews too. One of them, only an infant, is the apple of my eye. His name is Alden. After my dad." She told him how his mom said she'd fit in. "You will. The women rule the roost, as it should be. They're all, like you, very kick-ass and strong willed. Magical as well. I don't know that you'll get anything from being around them, but we'll cross that bridge when we get there. Will you come and sit with me?"

"Yes. In a second. What do you mean, they're strong willed? I'm not." He only had to cock a brow at her, and she could tell he didn't believe her. "I'm not. I'm very backward and shy. I don't like confrontations either. I avoid them whenever I can."

"Perhaps, but you also can take it on when necessary. As you did with Donna." She asked him who that was. "The drunk. You've been calling her Debby all day. I thought you were just having fun with her."

That made her laugh, hard. It felt so good that she got up and sat down beside Pierce on the couch. And when he picked her up and put her on his lap, she had no trouble with that either. The man was growing on her.

~*~

"I have a question for you. I mean before we get to other more interesting things." Pierce told her to ask away, but he didn't sit still, as she was sure she thought he would. Instead, he nibbled at her throat. Massaged her arms, legs, and whatever else he could touch of her. "You're not helping me."

"Good. Then my plan is succeeding." He stopped for a moment and stared at her. "What is more important than me having a little snack before we go back to your place and fool around?"

"That's it." He didn't know what she meant and asked her. "Why do I feel like you've just been there for me forever? Like my heart didn't beat right until I saw you? That nothing I do, say, or even try had any meaning until you came along and swept me up into...well, into you. It's like I didn't know what living was like until you came along and showed me."

"That is the most beautiful thing anyone has ever said to me." He held her to his chest. "I don't want to use the same old saying that is true of our kind by telling you that you and I were meant to be together, and that is why we both feel this way. It's more than that with you. I've seen my brothers fall in love with their mates, their mates eventually coming around to falling in love with them. But with you, just as you said, it's been there all along. We've only been waiting on one another to make the connection so our lives would have meaning. Purpose."

Joey sat up and looked at him. "There's more that I feel with you too, Pierce. I love you. I've never been in love before. Really, I've never thought it would be a thing I'd do, fall in love. I did think that someday I'd marry, but doubtfully for any other reason than that it was time. I needed the security. Or children. Do you want them?" He told her as many as she wanted. "See? Right there. That's what I'm talking about. You and I just click. I feel, to be honest with you, that soon the other shoe will drop, and this will all be gone. I don't want to lose you, Pierce. I need you as much as I do my next breath."

Pierce held her in his arms then. He wanted to shout to the world that she was perfect, that a mate like this didn't come around all the time. But holding her, for now, seemed like more than he could have ever hoped for. When the phone rang, neither of them moved to answer it. Pierce could tell when the cleaning crew got off the elevator a few minutes later. Their mixture of chemicals, dusting cloths, and the dinner they'd had was perfuming the air.

When Joey sat up and turned and looked at him, her smile was like the sun coming out after a heavy storm. Standing up when she did, he watched her as she turned off her computer, shut down the printer, and made sure her desk chair was under her desk.

He filled the fridge, making sure it had plenty of water for tomorrow. As they worked together, words weren't necessary. Pierce hadn't felt this comfortable around another being since he was a boy, not even sure if he could count his family in the comfort zone he was in now. When the lights were off to her office, he waited for the door to be closed before Piece pulled her back into his arms.

"How about some dinner? Then we can sit around and talk about whatever you want." She asked him about making love to her. "I'd love to make love with you. But there isn't any rush."

"Oh yes, there is. Buddy, I could take you where you stand. But there isn't enough room for me to do the things I want to that body of yours." She went to the elevator and pushed the button for down. He was still standing there, sure his mouth was hanging open and his tongue hanging out, as she stepped into the elevator shaft. "Well? Are you coming or not?"

"Not before you do." He nearly skipped to be with her. Even before the doors closed, Pierce had her pressed tightly against the wall, his mouth taking possession of hers as he slid his hand well up and under her skirt and beneath her tiny stringed panties. "Christ, you smell delicious. And you're so wet." He tore her panties off her and slipped them into his pocket.

Taking his soaking fingers to his mouth, he suckled all her cream off them as he watched her eyes. They were dark now, darkened because she wanted him as much as he did her. Pierce knew he had to be aware of his surroundings, at least enough so that they'd be able to come back tomorrow. He had to make sure she didn't get embarrassed or put in a position that would undoubtedly be all over the papers and social network. So pulling away, the hardest thing he'd ever done, Pierce leaned against the opposite wall just as the doors opened to the floor below them.

The couple that walked into the elevator with them nodded once, then turned their backs on them. He knew on some level that they could still see them—the brass of the walls, the lighting that was showing every corner. Breathing was difficult. His cock was painfully full. Staring at Joey, he set his mind on the tasks at hand.

They needed to get out of this building without making love on anything that had a hard surface. Of course, thinking of that, all he could think about was his cock and how hard it was. The way her panties were still in his pocket, the scent of her lingering on his hands. The way—

"This is our floor." Pierce had to shake the thoughts from his mind when Joey poked him in the chest. "We need to get out of this elevator and home, Pierce. Buck up, or we'll never make it."

"I'm all right with that." They walked to the doors that would put them on a busy street. Taking her hand into his, he held onto her tightly when the crowd around them seemed to engulf them in their path. Going to the parking garage, not ten feet away from where they were, Pierce kept telling himself to take a step, then another. To breathe. It was, he thought, the only thing he could center on for now.

The blur of getting to his car would haunt him for a few minutes. He not only had no idea how they'd gotten there so quickly, but how he'd even managed to unlock the door and hand Joey in. Getting into his side, Pierce put on his safety belt and put his hands on the steering wheel. A small laugh from Joey had him turning to look at her.

"Did you know you've been talking to yourself?" He asked her what he'd been saying. "'Take a step. One foot in front of the other. Breathe, you moron.' That one was my favorite. Like you might have forgotten how to do that."

"With you around, I'm not even sure I could do one of the simplest things I've done all my life." He smiled at her when she laughed again. "I love you, Joey. So very much. Will you marry me this weekend when we go to my parents' house? Make me the happiest man on earth by staying with me while I try to convince myself that I am truly your mate for all time?"

"I will." She leaned over and kissed him on the cheek. "Now. I'm not staying at my house because it's been bugged one too many times for me to trust it. So where are you staying? I'm assuming it's a hotel?" He shook his head and said it was a nice house. "All right. I'm starving. Not just for you, but for food too. I feel like I've not eaten in months."

Starting the car, he backed out of the parking space he'd been in. Even as he put it in gear, he asked her where she wanted to go. Deciding on a restaurant near his house, they headed that way. Christ, he thought, he had a mate. She loved him, and Pierce was going to get married as soon as Saturday. Sure, it was going to be just a filing of the certificate, but it would be legal. Neither of them wanted to chance having their big day ruined by things going on. Both of them had decided that if this was all they got, someone filing it away in the records, then they were fine with that.

"When I go to your home this weekend, remind me to take a kit." He told her he would if she told him what that was. "Designer kit I used when I was younger. It had bits and pieces of material in it that— I'm trying my best not to think about having you inside of me, and I need you to talk. About anything. I'm fucking going insane here."

Pierce laughed. He was still laughing when he pulled into the restaurant. Taking her hand into his, he kissed the back of it and guided her inside. For as much as he wanted her, he knew that without food, neither of them was going to survive the other. Ordering, they held hands. While they waited on their first course, they talked about going home. As they finished off their meals, they got to know one another better. It was as perfect as he'd seen in sitcoms, where it all comes together well, and all the dots are lined up flawlessly.

Joey would be his mate for all time. Taking this few hours to get to know one another also gave him time to calm his bear. By the time they were in the car and headed toward his house, both of them were at ease with each other. Joey commented on that as they entered the house.

"I'm in love with you too. I truly am. Had we gone straight to sex, I think I would have missed something so profoundly amazing about you." He asked her what that might have been. "That you're genuinely a very nice man."

"And you, my love, my heart, are the most astonishing person I've ever met. You're lovely, inside and out. You're generous, smart, and mine." He laughed. "Now, get naked before you have nothing else to wear."

Chapter 4

"What do you mean you're going to leave the country? Why? Is this because of my sister? Don't worry about her. She's not going to be anyone's trouble soon enough." Peter looked at her as she lay naked across his bed. Margie had been having an affair with him since long before her mother had refused to let her marry him. For more than ten years, as a matter of fact. "I am still trying to get information on where my mother is. But as of this morning, all my little spies have been taken out of the picture. I blame it on that bastard she hired recently."

"Harvey?" She said it was a younger man. She couldn't remember his name. "I was going to tell you that Harvey is harmless too. Your sister only hired him for a tax break, I think. You know you get a lot of breaks for hiring old people."

Margie didn't point out that he was older than Harvey. Peter was at least as old as her mom. Perhaps older, for all she knew. But they were happy together. And now that his wife was gone, hopefully dead, they could get busy in making things for them permanent. She brought up marrying him again.

"I mean, we're sure she's dead, right?" He said that without a body, there was no telling where the bitch was. "She never did anything anyone wanted her to do. And her mom was just a bitch to everyone. I can't believe you married her instead of me."

"I was going to marry you, but since your parents put a stop to it, I had to make myself respectable. Besides, marrying like I did, Rebecca couldn't tell on me. You wouldn't, even at the threat of death, but by me marrying her, Rebecca couldn't testify against me in a court of law. It was that or kill her like I did her father." It made sense, but she still didn't have to like it. "Also, you might not have realized this, but with her out of the picture right now, I don't have to worry so much about her and that brat. Christ, that kid could get on a man's last nerve."

When Peter got out of the bed, she turned her head away from his nudity. She loved the man, but his body wasn't all that pretty anymore. She didn't think it had been since she'd been sleeping with him. The man was old, but he was rich and all hers. Taking a peek at him, just to see if anything had changed, she waited until he got into the shower before getting up herself.

Gray hairs stuck out all over his chest like spiny needles. His hair was falling out on his head. Even his dick, as impressive as it was, didn't stand up as well as it used to. Sometimes she'd have to fake her own pleasure so he'd get off her. He was also overweight.

"Did you want to have something to eat before you leave?" She asked him if she was leaving. "Yes. You told me you had to see to something with your sister. Don't you remember that?"

"Yes. Her business. I have to find someone I can blackmail into getting information on her. I have to tell you, Peter, she's getting a lot more mistrustful of late. Did I tell you I can't even get a rise out of her when I try and piss her off?" He said she had — several times. "Well, it bears repeating. Mom too. She only stares at me like she's looking for a place to put a knife."

"She's about due for another payment. That'll come in handy." That was another thing about Peter that had surprised her — he wasn't rich. He had money, show money, he told her, but the real cash was in offshore accounts for their golden years. "Also, that Blake character is late. Again. I'm going to have to send someone after him."

Pulling on her robe, she went to the bathroom when he came out. It nearly made her puke every time she had to follow him in the bathroom. His hair was in the tub and on the sink, and he never hit the toilet. Careful not to step in his pee, she turned on the water as hot as it would go so that she could at least get some of the little things he'd left behind.

She asked herself the same question she did every time she came here. *Why are you still in love with him?* She didn't know anymore. In fact, Margie wasn't even sure she liked him all that much. He was a slob, uncaring of her feelings, and usually, a great deal lately, he'd break plans with her in order to do some kind of job that needed him. Stepping into the shower after adjusting the temperature, she leaned against the stall wall and let her tears fall.

So why stay with him? The voice again. She'd thought at first it was her own thoughts intruding on her day. But it told her it wasn't herself she was reasoning with, but someone with a great deal of power. *I mean, it's not like he even takes you out to dinner anymore. The last time you had any fun with him, including sex, was when you shot Rebecca and left her for dead.*

We surely did celebrate that night. The voice asked her how long it had been before that. *Plenty. Why are you bothering me again? I thought I told you to get the hell out of my head.*

I thought since there is plenty of room up here, as you don't seem to have a brain, you'd not mind so much. Have you always been a bitch, Margie? I mean, doing the exact opposite of what you were told all the time? Staying where you knew no one wanted you to be? I guess you've not always been a bitch. Babies aren't, I guess. But pretty much all of your adult life. She asked her what she wanted. *Oh, you don't want to know what I want from you, Margie. I'm just here to keep you thinking about things I know you'd rather not. Such as the fact that the man you're fucking has three other women that join him in that big bed you've just gotten out of. Also, I do believe there have been a couple of men in that bed. No women with them, just men. Not that it matters, I suppose, but you should know he has better staying power with them than he does with you.*

Deciding to ignore the voice in favor of having a nice dinner with Peter before she left, Margie dressed in something killer. Her body certainly looked good in red, she thought as she looked in the mirror. However, the voice didn't stop talking.

Putting on a little weight there, aren't you? I mean, you're supposed to have curves, but they don't curve out in front of you. It's supposed to be down your sides. She told the voice to shut up. *I'm just saying. You're getting very fat.*

"I'm not fat." Peter asked her who she was talking to. "No one. I'm just telling myself I've not put on any weight since high school."

"Not that it matters, but you have sort of started sagging a little — a little jigglier than you were before. I guess we all do when we get older. I used to be a slim bastard. Now I'm just a bastard." Margie stared at Peter as he slapped her on the ass. "You still have it as far as I'm concerned, however, Margie dear. Always good for a nice fuck."

See? He thinks you're a nice fuck, when I know for a fact he told the two men he had last night that they were fantastic fucks. The voice laughed. *I'm thinking in a few more months, less perhaps, you're going to be tossed aside, and he'll be having someone…what did he call it? Oh, yeah. Less jiggly.*

It hurt her on levels she didn't understand that this voice was playing on her insecurities. It could have been her own thoughts, but the voice had proven her wrong on that score late last night. It had woke her from her sleep and had her in the kitchen making a bowl of cereal for herself—something she'd not had since she was a child—that she didn't know where the stuff had come from.

Leaving the house without speaking to anyone, especially Peter, she made her way to her own home. She did hope he was sitting in his house wondering what the hell had become of her when they were supposed to be going out to dinner. The dress was off and torn to shreds even before she was all the way up the stairs to her bedroom. She would never wear it again, so shredding it the way she had made her feel a little better. Pulling out a pair of soft pants and a T-shirt, she sat down at her vanity and looked at herself in the mirror.

She and Joey were twins. Joey was twenty-three minutes older than her, but it had always been Margie that looked older. Not just the twenty-three minutes, but more like twenty-three years. Margie hadn't aged well, she thought. Even for as young as she knew she was, she looked terrible. Old and worn out.

Supposing it had to do with the way she lived, even trying to be good and exercise hadn't changed her looks one bit. It had been a thought for her for some time to get some plastic surgery, a tuck or two here, and a bit of fat sucked out there. But it was much more expensive than she'd dreamed it would have been. And asking for the money to do that from Peter or her sister was just a humiliation she didn't want to risk.

Making sure there wasn't anyone at the offices, she called three times. Every time someone answered from the service her sister employed, she was put on hold so they could take a message. She didn't want to talk to anyone. She just wanted to find out if she could go there and mess things up a bit.

You can't. Just so you know. The voice again. Asking her what she was talking about, the voice told her she'd not be able to get into the building anymore. *Because as of the moment they left for the day, a pack of angry wolves made their way to the property and has been keeping an eye on things for them. You're shit out of luck in having your kind of fun, I guess. It really helped me hire them when I told them who they were guarding the place against. Not too nice to shifters, are you?*

I fucking loathe them. Voice asked her how they'd hurt her. *Can you imagine having sex with one of them, and they suddenly turn into this great wolf or something? I do not do doggie sex. That's fucking insane.*

That's really too bad for you, then. I mean, I have a bear in my bed every night. Kinda fun, if in a kinky sort of way. And they certainly do have a great deal more endurance than the old paunch belly you're fucking now. Voice laughed. *I've decided to tell you my first name. That way, you don't have to keep referring to me as The Voice. While that sounds all mystical and shit, I do have a real name. You can call me Meadow.*

Maybe I like calling you The Voice. She told her whatever floated her turds. *It's boat, not turds, you moron. Christ, you'd think I was the only intelligent one on this earth.*

Doubtful anyone would think you're even remotely intelligent, Margie. I mean, you've been fucking the same man for at least the last ten years. Have you ever once had a good climax? The kind that makes your voice hurt for days after screaming it out? Or been so sore from how hard you were taken that you smile at every little twinge? You've been lacking. That's all I can tell you. Lacking in getting a good fuck since you were fourteen years old. So very sad, if you ask me. She told her she'd not asked. *Oh well. You've not had real sex until you've been with a man your own age who has a dick that stands up to attention when you simply enter a room.*

When The Voice—she refused to call her by name—shut up for a while, Margie got her things gathered up while waiting on a pizza to be delivered for her supper. She was going to go on a diet tomorrow, she told herself. As soon as this thing with Peter and that brat was finished, she'd be eating less due to not being stressed all the time. Her dinner came about the time she was looking at the exercise equipment she'd purchased several years ago with the intention of getting in shape. Now it was mostly used as a discarded clothing rack. She would have to do something soon, she told herself, or she'd never like herself.

Margie drove over to the building her sister used and found that it looked as abandoned as it normally did. However, as soon as she got out of the car, a pack of wolves surrounded the place. She wondered if she could kill them all when the number of them doubled, their beady eyes staring at her like they knew she was going to be a tasty treat.

"Shoo. Go away." Margie was sure they were laughing at her. "You don't want to see me take you on, you little shits. Go away so I can go into my sister's business."

I'm translating for you for the pack leader. Margie asked the voice why they didn't just talk to her directly. *Because in order to do that, he'd have to have to bite you. I think any one of them wouldn't stop at just a little nibble. Anyway, he said to tell you that if you come within fifteen feet of the building, you'll never make it one step closer. I don't think he likes you overly much.*

Good. I don't care for him either. I will get in. Voice told her to go for it. *You just keep it up, Voice, and I'm going to hunt you down.*

The laughter startled her—not only that, but it made the hair on her arms stand up. There wasn't a bit of humor in it. Nothing but malice and contempt. Like this person knew more than she would ever know about killing people.

You have no idea what I'm capable of, Margie. The

things I've done to people I dislike. You're one of those people. But for now, I'm having fun with you. Jerking you around, you might call it. The woman that appeared in front of her scared Margie enough that she fell to the ground, her face a nightmarish one that made her ill. "This is a warning you can heed or not. Leave them alone. Leave the little girl alone too, or else — I'm going to show you what I'm going to do to you. Just to show that I mean business. However, you can bet I'm going to enjoy driving you over the edge."

Margie found herself at home. She hadn't any idea how she got there. After the woman showed her how she was going to kill her, Margie didn't remember anything else. The playing of her death, in so many different ways, sickened her.

Sitting in the darkening room, she tried to convince herself it had been a nightmare. That she'd fallen asleep. But every time she moved on the chair she was on, with every little, tiny movement of her legs, she could feel the pain of falling to the ground when the woman had startled her. That, if nothing else, made it perfectly clear it wasn't a dream.

Making her way to the front hall, she stood there for several seconds, just staring at the open door. Driving her over the edge. It was working, Margie thought. The sight of the wolf standing there, his fur standing up on end, had her rethinking her entire life up until now. Meadow, or whatever the fuck her name was, would do just as she said. Of that, she had no doubt.

Going back into the living room, she turned every light on in the room. The wolf, the one at the door, must have closed the door behind him as she heard it shut. When he came in, getting up on the couch across from her, Margie started laughing. It was that she thought or put a bullet in her own head. Things were getting very scary for her.

~*~

Joey was nervous. Not about having sex or making love, as he called it, but in disappointing him. Pierce had to have had sex more than she had. More than likely, all the —

"Stop thinking so hard." She smiled at him, and he grinned back at her. "I don't know what you're thinking, but nothing could be as bad as you're making it out to be. Nothing in this room or any other time that we're together will happen unless you want it to. I promise you that on the heart of my mom."

"You're saying that if I were to walk around this room completely naked and then tell you I didn't want to have sex, you'd be all right with that?" He didn't even hesitate—he told her that was right. "I haven't any idea why, but I believe you. You're much too nice to me."

"I love you." She nodded and sat on the edge of the bed. "What do you want to happen? Do you want to make love? Would you rather just sleep?"

"I want very much to make love with you. But I'm

afraid of you having much more experience than me, and I'm not up to par with you." She asked him if he understood. He told her he didn't think that was going to be right. "You do have more experience than I do. You have to know that."

"What I do know is that you're about as nervous as I've ever seen you. It's sort of cute if you ask me." Pierce stood up and started to unbutton his shirt. "However, I don't want to think of you being cute when all I can really think about is having you naked beneath me while I'm pounding you with my cock."

"Right to the point. I like that about a man." She unbuttoned the buttons on her blouse while he still stood a few feet from her. "I will tell you I'm very noisy when I have a climax. I think that got around — that you couldn't just…you know, have a quicky with me in the corner. Not that I ever did that, but…well, men do talk."

"I wouldn't say a word about how you come. To anyone." He had his shirt off, and it dropped onto the floor. "I want you to make all the noise you want. The louder, the better. If we were out in the woods, my bear would roar out his own release when I come. I'm not entirely sure how that works, but then I've never made love to my mate before."

"Is it different?" Pierce paused in undoing his pants and looked to be thinking about it. "Never mind. I'm assuming you'd not know that either since you've never had a mate before. Why is that?"

"Why is what?" She asked him. "From legends, it's said that creatures like us, shifters, can only have a single one that they can love. They love with all they are, never leaving room for anyone else but their children to intrude in their lives. Family doesn't count—I asked. Now, I do know that the fates, creatures we believe in, will take a person that has lost his or her mate and find them another. It's said that a creature lucky enough to find someone to love, then a second time, is well and truly blessed by the gods that care for such matters."

"That's beautiful." She pulled off her skirt and looked down at herself. "I seemed to have lost my panties someplace."

She was standing in her bra only, one she'd created that left very little to the imagination. Joey had an entire drawer full of them. They gave her a boost of confidence more than anything she'd ever made. But the way Pierce was staring at her, his boxer briefs barely holding onto his hard cock, she found herself wanting to cover up from head to toe.

"Don't." She put her hands down along her sides when he told her to stop. It wasn't the word he used that had her wet—it was the growl in his voice. The way his bear, the black fur of him, seemed to run over his skin. "You're lovely. No, that's not right. I don't think a word has ever been made that would describe the beauty I'm seeing before me."

"Oh, Pierce, you're wonderful with words." She

took a step toward him, slowly, in the event that he asked her to stop. "I'm betting for every wonderful romantic word that flows past your lips, your hands and body are ten times more devastating to a girl."

"Only you." His words, like before, struck her body like a well-aimed bow, touching her heart and soul like nothing else could have. Or would, she'd bet. "I want to taste you."

Putting action to words, he dropped to his knees before her, pulling her body to his face. She screamed out the first climax she'd had in a very long time. But instead of letting her fall to the floor—it had taken that much out of her—Pierce ate her like a man on his last meal. His tongue moved inside of her like she was sure his cock would, filling her and pounding her clit like he was literally making love to her with it. Each time she came, he would growl again, bringing her over the edge so many times she was weak with it. Finally, pulling away from him, Joey staggered to the bed.

"I'm finished." He was standing over her now, his body hard with his need. "Or perhaps not. Christ, will you even fit in me? I want to taste you as well."

"You put your mouth on me, and I'm never going to get to take you the way you deserve. As it is right now, even the thought of being inside of you has me so close to coming I'm afraid to touch you." Her heart flittered again. "Baby, I'm sorry."

Before she could ask him what he was sorry for, he

filled her—from her pussy to her throat, she could feel his cock there. Even though it had been a painful entry, she wanted more. All of him. Wrapping her legs around him when he leaned over her, she pulled his mouth to hers as her body slowly adjusted to his.

"Christ, I love you." As soon as he moved, just moving his hips on the bed, she came hard. Her eyes rolled to the back of her head, and she was sure she could see stars. "I'm going to move us up on the bed."

Whatever he wanted to do, she was fine with it. Every little movement, from his fingers or his body, would send her off. At this rate, she was going to be nothing but a puddle of skin when he finished with her. When he laughed, she realized she was thinking out loud.

"I promise you, love, I'll never leave you a puddle of anything." He moved again, adjusting them so they fit where he wanted them. Thankful that the bed was huge, she decided she was never going to have a headache where this man was concerned. Joey doubted she'd ever have to fake anything with Pierce in her arms.

In the middle of the bed, he made love to her body, touching parts of her that she didn't remember having. Awakening her skin to new and delicious sensations she loved. His moans told her he was enjoying this as much as she was. Even after coming so many times, so many wonderful, fulfilling times, she knew the one she needed was yet to hit her.

Pierce spoke to her, not with words but by worshiping her. His mouth paid homage to her breasts, ribs, and earlobes even as he moved inside of her, taking her to the highest of peaks only to bring her down slowly.

Joey touched him as well. Licking at his flesh so that she could taste him, she discovered she loved the taste of him. The way his sweat tasted so warm as it lay on her tongue. Even his nipples, hard as tiny stones, had an appeal to her she'd never thought of before.

"Mark me, Joey. Make me yours." While she didn't know what he might have meant by that before making love to him, all she wanted to do now was bite him. To taste his blood as it flowed from his body. Nuzzling his neck, she could feel the pulse there, pounding against her tongue as she found where she wanted to mark him.

Dragging her teeth over it, she felt Pierce shudder. When she sank her teeth into his neck, his blood filling her mouth, he held her to him as he cried out his own release. Joey felt like she was being turned inside out. Her body shattered and came back together, with parts of Pierce filling her out. Even as she drank greedily of him, she came again and again.

"Again." She had no idea if he could come again but wanted it. More than she did anything in the world, she wanted to feel him filling her again. When he threw back his head and roared out, she saw the bear inside of him rolling over him. It was by far the most erotic thing she'd ever witnessed. Then she came.

Never in the history of sex would anyone have been able to prepare her for her release. Such a tame word for what happened to her. Even as she was being tossed around in the vortex of her mind and body, she knew on some level that this wasn't normal. This was extraordinary.

Her mind blinked out when thoughts, memories of his, came to her. Joey felt the small cuts to his body he'd done when younger. The pride he took in his work for Demi and the others. Not only did she see him there, but she was also sure he was seeing her as well.

When he collapsed atop her, Joey didn't care that he was crushing her. She could have died for all she cared. Her body would be found days from now with a sated smile on her face and her entire body limp with sex. Closing her eyes as Pierce rolled them over to his back, sleep didn't just take her, but it ran her down and took over.

Waking up, the room was dark. They'd not drawn the curtains, but she could tell someone had. Reaching for Pierce, she came up off the bed when his side of the bed was cold. He was sitting at the little table, looking at what appeared to be a laptop.

"Are you seriously working right now? How the hell do you have even the slightest bit of energy for something like that." He turned and grinned at her. When he wiggled his brows, she laughed. "What has you so interested that you had to get out of this nice bed and leave me here to freeze? I just realized how warm you are."

"Your sister. She's been arrested." She got up, wrapping a blanket around her, and went to sit on his lap. "Meadow reached me and told me I had to look into it. She didn't want you to find out when we went into work today. They're saying she was trying to set fire to Peter's home. There aren't a lot of details just yet."

"She tried to burn down Peter's home? Christ, I wonder what happened between them that she'd do something like that. She's been in love with the prick since we were children." There was a video of her being arrested that she watched twice. "Do you suppose she's stoned? She looks like she's out of it."

"Drunk. I guess after she left your building earlier this evening—or I guess yesterday now—she went home and did some heavy drinking. I didn't know she lived alone. Anyway, she got drunk and decided to go talk to Peter about a few things. Whatever they are, she's not telling the police." She asked if she'd been hurt. "Not that they're saying. But they would have taken her to the hospital had she been. Peter is pressing charges."

"Of course he is. The bastard is old enough to be her father, and he's been sleeping with her since she was barely old enough to cross the street on her own. Mom said she'd tried her best to keep them apart, but nothing ever worked. Does it mention Rebecca or Becky?" He said it didn't. When he didn't say any more, she looked at him. "Tell me. I have a feeling it wasn't just this arrest that had you up at this ungodly hour."

"No. There is more. Nothing that can't wait if you don't want to hear it." She told him she wanted to hear it. "All right. Meadow is very powerful. I've mentioned this to you before. Today she was able to break into Margie's mind while she was drunk and found out a few things that could potentially have her put in prison. She killed Rebecca. Margie not only pulled the trigger, but she also tried to kill Becky. Getting them out of the way so she could be with Peter has been her goal since Peter married the other woman. There have been other murders she's committed. She's sort of the hitman of choice for Peter, I guess you could say."

"Does anyone else know about this? I mean, her killing Rebecca? Like my mom?" Pierce hesitated, and her mind went all over the place. "She does, doesn't she?"

"I don't know that she knows for certain, but she does know that Margie has killed before. Some people that had— I guess for lack of a better way to put it, people that tried to tell her she couldn't do things. Like, be a killer. Be married to Peter. She also doesn't care to be proven wrong. People around her don't last when they point that out to her." Joey asked him if he had this sort of information on Peter. "Peter is a homosexual. That is something he tries to hide from everyone, but Meadow found out and told Margie he was never going to marry her. That he prefers men over a woman. Also, Peter is a very wealthy man, but not in this country. Meadow is looking into getting his account information now. She told me it would be enough for Becky to be able to get help if she needs it, as well as college money. It's something she's done before for victims."

Wrapping the blanket around her tighter, the chill of the information she was getting made her slightly ill. She didn't want to think about things that were going on, but she had a feeling it was going to be worse before it got better.

"Would you like to go home today? And take me with you? I don't want to be at work for the next few days until I can get my head wrapped around all this. I'm sure it's not going to end nicely for anyone, but I'd very much like to meet your family, get married, and have some fun." Pierce told her that was what he was going to suggest. "I'll call Harvey and have him take care of things for me. There is enough they can do there for today, and they can have Friday off. With pay."

"Something I've been meaning to tell you. I don't know what your finances are like, but I have enough that you'd not have to work if you didn't want to. I know you enjoy your job and you're very good at what you do. But now that we're together, whatever I have is now yours. I also have a big house." She asked him about children. "As many as you want to give me. By your body or adoption, I'm game if you are. Even kidnapping one if you'd like."

"How about we stick to the standard way of getting

children, by me getting pregnant or adoption. I like your body too much to think we'd have that much fun in a prison cell." She got dressed and hated that she'd have to wear her same clothing. "I might have to bring a duffle all the time if we're going to be going other places."

"Think of what you want to wear. I don't know for sure that it'll work for you, but— Well, I guess it does." She was blown away at how easy it was to be dressed. "It's a mate thing. Madden can't do it yet, but once he finds his mate, he'll be able to do it as well."

She was thinking of all the applications she could use this particular trick on while they ran by her building. The kits she wanted to take home for his nieces were ready to go. They were on the road toward the airport by the time the sun was coming up. She was so happy she forgot for a while that she was hiding out. Joey was so excited about seeing his family that she'd almost forgotten she'd be seeing her mom too.

Chapter 5

Demi watched Joey with the girls. To say she was in her element would have been a gross understatement. All the kids sitting around the massive table with their eyes glued to their new aunt was just what they all needed. And she was impressed as hell that they didn't think she was stupid for having them dress dolls with their creations. Lucian came up behind her while she was standing there.

"I just left, Dad. He said to tell you he's going to take the baby home with him, and he'd make you come to visit him." She laughed. It had been the same threat he'd given her this morning when she'd come into the living room to find him telling her son that his mommy was a fighter. "What going on with that?"

"He said I'm selfish with his namesake. Something about having to come all the way over here to have a manly talk with him. I told him as soon as he could prove to me that he could lactate, he could take him overnight. I think I embarrassed him." Lucian laughed, and the girls smiled at him. "I don't think the kids are ever going to live with their parents again. They're having the time of their lives right now. Even Jilly, who I didn't think would want to be a part of making clothing. But as Joey pointed out, she had to wear them, so why not come up with something comfy and functional too." They made their way into the living room. "Tomorrow, I'm going to take Joey over to a couple of buildings we own. I have a feeling she's going to be moving here with not just her business, but everything, as soon as possible. The rent she's paying for the one she's in now is really eating away at her profit margin."

"I'm thinking she'll like the one next to the old Cameron building. You know which one that is?" She did and hadn't thought of that. "If we really do end up taking the Cameron building down, she'll be able to expand too. I saw Meadow telling her about the shipping equipment she had left over after renovations were done at the plant out on Forty."

"I love that idea. And she and Pierce will be close to all of us. I did worry about that, her moving him to New York." Lucian said he had as well. "I have a question for you. What do you think of her mom?"

"Lauren, Joey's mom? I don't know. I don't talk to her all that much. I think she's mostly in hiding." Demi said that was just it. She didn't have to hide while there. "Did she say why she wasn't coming over? I'd think she'd be right here now that you mention it."

"She's embarrassed." Pierce walked up and handed her a large glass of juice, then winked at her as he continued. "Her daughter, Margie, found out a few things about her that has her too embarrassed to show herself to us. She's thinking that all your kindness, it's only because I'm going to marry Joey."

"That's the most stupid thing…I guess I can understand it. But you go and get her and bring her here. I mean, it is your house anyway." Pierce winked at her again as he walked away. "Love sure does look good on him, don't you think? I mean, he's not even touching the floor when he walks. When are the others coming over? I have his license all fixed up for tomorrow. But we're going to have dinner here tonight, right?"

"Yes." She sat down on the couch and watched as Alden took a nap with her baby on his chest. They'd both be well rested when they woke up, and she couldn't think of a safer place for either of them to be. "Do you suppose he'll be like this with all the babies? I mean, talking to them as if they have a clue what he tells them?"

"Pretty much. I just spoke to Alan. He is coming over tonight since we'll all be here. Also, Gaea is going to show up. They want to give the rewards to Lucy and Ian. How well do you think that is going to go over?" She told him it wouldn't at all. "I didn't think so. Alan told me the other day that he was getting his finances in order. You don't think he's planning to off himself, do you?"

"No. I mean, I don't think he would. But he did

tell me it had been centuries since he'd taken a look at his portfolio. I look at ours daily, but to go centuries without even peeking at it would make me crazy." They both laughed as she drank her juice. Setting the glass by the couch arm, she wasn't surprised to see it fill again. "I wonder if we were to pool all of our magic how much damage we could really do."

"Why do you ask?" Lucian sounded so suspicious she had to laugh. "Joey was telling my mom that she is so excited about the clothing thing. She has been trying on the different colors with outfits the girls come up with—sort of a demo mode. Cybill is loving every second of this. Just as I knew she would."

Closing her eyes, she must have fallen asleep. The next thing she remembered was the voice of Alan in the other room. Getting up, she noticed that not only was her son awake, but so was Alden. The two of them were watching something on television. She thought it was a game but didn't look at it long enough to figure it out.

"She's stubborn." Demi kissed Alan on the forehead and told him they all were. "Yes, but she must take this gift for saving my life. I have worked very hard on it."

The rest of the family was there now, including Lauren. She was talking to Becky, and that made her happy. The woman would just have to realize that her daughter wasn't any different than any of the other family members each of them had.

"Lucy, take the damned gift." Lucy started to tell her she didn't want to be rewarded for killing a man. "Would you rather he had killed Alan or any of the other people in this room? I didn't think so. Now, take the gift, and we'll move on. I'm to understand that Gaea is going to be here as well sometime this evening. Please."

"All right. But it had better not be something huge." Alan just laughed. "I'm serious. It wasn't hard for me to kill him, thanks to you. And the fact that we're getting rewarded twice for his death is almost too much for me."

Everyone gathered in the living room. Just as Alan cleared his throat, Gaea materialized in the room as well. When she bowed before them all, Alan smiled at her. Thanking her for her help, he turned to Lucy and Ian.

"As you all know, I'm a very old and very powerful vampire. It isn't often that I put myself in a position that might get me killed. My only thought that afternoon was to give Lucy whatever she needed in the way of magic to keep herself safe from the monster that had tried to trick them." Hollie had too, Demi remembered. He'd tried to make it so Ian and Lucy finished out his life sentences in prison. It had been a mess. "It did and still does amaze me that someone so giving and so wonderful wouldn't allow someone to repay her kindness. Well, I'm happy to say that today I get to repay her."

"You don't have to do anything. I want you to be aware of that." Lucy hugged Alan when he said he understood that. "You're a very nice person. Vampire or not, I would have saved you anyway."

"I know that as well, my dear. It's what makes me so happy to be able to do this for you and yours. I have worked for some of the nicest people. Some not so much, but working with the McCray family gave me more than a reason to live, but a reason to be a good man. The bruin here have become family to me as well. More than I ever dreamed possible when I was set upon this world as a creature of the night. Now. I know this family well enough to know that no matter how small a gift I gave, it would be something that they share. I've taken that into consideration when I thought about the gift for you. I have magic to give to you first. It is the gift of immortality. I cannot give you the gift of complete immortality because I can still be killed by silver."

"That's wonderful." Lucy hugged him and thanked him several times. He told her he wasn't finished. "That is more than enough. I know some of the family has this already, but it's nice to know we'll all be around for a long time."

"Yes, but even with all the life in the world, there will still be issues. And that is the second part of my gift to you. I wish for you all to have all that I am. I am keeping my home and the contents for now, but should anything untoward happen to me, I'd like to think you'd make good use of it, as you will this money I have given you today." Lucy looked at Demi, then back at Alan. Even she didn't understand what that was. "I have given Alden and Cindy McCray, as well as their six sons, my finances, save what is in the house. Divided equally between the seven of you so that you'd not have to ever worry about money again. You can use it for whatever you wish, but I know you'll be using it for the good of the world."

"We don't worry about money now, Alan." He said he understood that, but he had no more use for money than he did a steak dinner. "I don't understand. You're not going to leave us, are you? I wouldn't be at all happy with you if that is your reason for doing this."

"No. I have no intentions of leaving you—ever, if you'll have me. No. I have more than enough money in my home that I don't have to worry about that either. However, what does an old vampire need that he cannot get on his own?" He kissed Lucy on the cheek. "You have, in one swift move, given me more than anyone has ever given me before. A purpose. A life."

Gaea stood up when Alan sat down.

"Wait. I don't understand." Ian looked around the room as the beautiful woman sat back down. "What do you mean, you've given us your all? Your money? Or magic? Either one of those seems to be something you'd need in your coming days. And I don't want you to leave us any more than anyone in this room does. What exactly are you meaning by your all?"

Alan laughed and put out his hand. When Ian took it, the room brightened up with the power that was there. As soon as he was able to release his hand, Ian fell backward. Looking more dazed than hurt, he told them he was fine. Lucy asked Alan what he'd done.

"I gave him what he wanted. The exact accounting of what I have gifted you." Ian was nodding, his face a little paler than she thought it should have been for a simple transfer of information. That made Demi laugh. "Would anyone else like to know what he knows?"

Everyone moved back, putting their hands behind them as they shook their heads. It would have been funny if not so serious. Ian promised he'd let them know verbally if they needed information. Laughing, Alan sat down beside Ian but didn't touch him again. Gaea stood again and smiled at them all.

"Mine isn't a gift, but a reward for the help in the killing of Hollie." She sat down and stood up again. "You have it. It's been, as with Alan's gift, given to each of you. Unlimited use of white magic that will do more for you than you've ever desired before. Also, you have immortality against everything now. Even Alan. You will find your reward from Alan in the form of a large chest at each of your homes."

That was it, apparently, because when she sat back down, everyone was called to dinner. This was the strangest day she'd ever had, she thought. Immortality for all of them? Magic out the ass? Whatever was going on, she wondered if they'd all get it or just the sons. Not that the money mattered, but she wanted to be around as long as Lucian would be.

"Everyone that comes to this family, by heart or body, will have what has been given to them by me. Even the things you have been given before, it too will be a part of the McCray legacy." She asked Gaea about the people they didn't want to have it. "Then they shan't. You will all be able to decide who will be here forever for you and those who will not. If you're speaking of the sister of Joey, then no, she will not be an immortal. Not unless things change. Which I'm not sure will. There are some things even I cannot see well enough to make a judgment call on them."

They were all surrounding the table, filling plates as large bowls came around. Demi had a moment to realize there might not be enough food when the bowl of corn on the cob was passed to Lucian. It was then she could see that it was refilling itself. Looking across the table to see if anyone else had noticed, she could see that Joey had. She looked at her with astonishment written all over her face.

"You learn to roll with it after a while." Nodding, the bowl in her hand was passed to Pierce. He was too busy talking to his dad to see what was literally right in front of him. "I take it this is all new to you as well?"

"Yes. I mean, we've only been staying here since Thursday night. The woman in the kitchen said she'd be able to whip something up at a moment's notice. I didn't know she meant magically." Demi told her it might well be her doing it. "No. Not today. I mean, it might be, but today I'm blaming it squarely on the cook. This is me easing into this. By the way, I have a lot of dresses, like dressy dresses, at home that I've designed over the years. Sometimes I have to make something so totally out of my comfort range in order to do work with the genre I do. If you or the other women would like them, you're more than welcome to them. In fact, anything in my line, it's yours. I can even do alterations if they need it."

"Really?" Joey nodded as she passed the next platter to her right. "I have to admit, I'd never heard of you before Cybill told me who you were. I don't exactly go out all that much where I have to dress up, and I think that is what I was thinking about when I thought of a designer. Someone who does those outlandish outfits I see on magazine covers."

"I worked for one of the high end designers when I first started out. The clothing wasn't as bad as I've seen, but it really didn't inspire me to go out and purchase it. When I left that firm, I was told I'd never make it on my own designing for the everyday woman. While a little more expensive than things you can pick up at a department store, they're very well made and sturdy. I have people passing down their clothing to their children." She asked her about the dolls and the scraps of material. "I think that was when I discovered I wanted to get colors together that most people wouldn't dream of. My grannie was forever making quilts, and she'd give me the scraps she didn't use. My dolls had the most colorful clothing ever conceived."

"The color of her pants are pumpkin pie, of all things." Demi told Lauren she didn't think of pie when she saw them. "Me either. But it works with a great many other colors I love. Purple is big right now, but it looks good with blues and reds. While I like bold statement colors together, Joey likes earth tones and calming colors. I think that is why we work so well together on this."

They talked about a lot of different things while eating. When the men were finished, they stood to clear the table while the women didn't move. Demi liked this. The women of the house to be able to linger at the table while the men usually went into the living room or outside. She was just sipping her tea when she heard a phone ringing in the house. Whoever it was for, Demi hoped no one would be called away. This was just too lovely of a thing to give up right now.

"Pierce and I were talking about me moving my business here. It wouldn't be a large undertaking, I'm thinking. Mostly it's bolts of material, which can be heavy, as well as a few cutting tables. The people I have working for me now are set to retire or not move if I were to go. Just Harvey. He's willing to work anywhere for me, he told me." Mel told Joey of the three buildings in the downtown area she thought would make a good storefront for her. "I've never sold direct before. Just online. That would be an entirely new concept for me."

"We'll help you. And I'm sure you have your first employees with Cybill and the other girls. They have really enjoyed what you brought them." Joey said she'd gotten a lot of ideas from them as well. "Good. I'm so glad Pierce found you. As I think it has been pointed out to you before, you're going to be a good fit with us."

"Right now, I'm not sure what that might mean. But as you said, we'll roll with it." She looked in the direction of the living room, where the men were screaming at a game on the television. "I feel like I have loved him forever. Does that make sense? We just came together like we were meant to be. He calms me."

"You more than likely calm him as well." Joey nodded and smiled at her. Demi thought it was a beautiful smile and couldn't help but smile back at her. "I like you, Joey. I do hope we have a lot of fun in the years to come."

"I like you too. You're just like Pierce said you were." She wanted to ask her what he'd said but didn't when she laughed. "It's all good. All of the things he'd said about you guys. I believe he's afraid of you too. More so his mom."

They talked and laughed for hours, moving from the table to the parlor-like room next to the living room. Once in a while, one of the men would come in, grab a kiss, ask them if they needed anything, then go back. This was, Demi thought, one of the most enjoyable evenings she'd spent with this family.

The fact was that it could have been stressful,

talking about Hightower and his plans for Becky. They could have also discussed Margie and the trouble she was going to be up against soon. But no one brought any of it up. No one seemed inclined, as she was not, to bring any negativity to the dinner and evening they were all enjoying. Demi thought they needed to do this more often. Leave the day outside of their family time together. It made for a very fun night out.

~*~

While she sat in the jail cell pondering her life, Margie wondered why things kept happening to her that were out of her control. Unlike her sister—Joey had always had things fall in her lap, and she'd be able to make something of herself. She had worked really hard at her job, but so had Margie. Getting Peter to marry her had been all she'd thought of since she'd been a little girl.

Margie wasn't unaware of the fact that Peter was old enough to be her father—even her grandfather, she supposed. The age difference never bothered her. He was just a mature man that needed someone younger around him all the time. At least up until recently—that was what she'd been telling herself. Lying on the cot, she looked up at the ceiling and wondered, not for the first time, how they got all those holes in each of the tiles up there without the thing falling apart.

Peter had taken her under his wing when she was twelve. Her father had died by then. Cancer had taken him away from her even though she'd begged him to get better. Her dad had been her everything, and she his world. Then he'd died and left her what she had thought of as a sea of uncertainties. Of things left undone. Not that she understood then what that meant, but it was the feeling she'd gotten upon his death.

Peter seemed to understand her better than anyone else had. The first time Peter had shown her any attention was at her dad's funeral. He'd taken her in the kitchen and talked to her while she ate a large piece of cake. Feeling really sleepy afterwards, she'd woken up in her bed naked. To this day, she had no idea what she'd done to get herself like that but was too ashamed to ask anyone. After that day, Peter would seek her out after school. Sometimes he'd even take her out for the day so they could be together.

Of course, her mom never noticed or cared enough to notice that she was getting out of class more and more. Mom had taken it hard when Dad died. So did Joey. But no one had rescued them as Peter did her. He'd not only taken her places they enjoyed going to, but he showed her all kinds of things, sexual things, that made her feel so adult with him.

She knew on a lot of levels it was wrong. But he was her hero, her lover, and the best man she'd ever been around, including her dad. Again, up until just recently. Thinking about what the voice had told her, she wondered if she could ask her something that had been bothering her. When she felt the small nudge at her mind, she turned to see who had poked her. There wasn't anyone there.

I'm here to answer anything you want. But you need to be aware that I don't hold back. I'm going to tell you the truth, and that's all. I don't sugarcoat anything when I'm being asked direct questions. Got it? She told her she did. *Also, before someone thinks you're nuttier than a fruit cake, you don't have to speak out loud to talk to me. Just answer me in your mind as you would a thought.*

Is he really gay? Instead of giving her an answer, she showed her Peter having sex with two men in the bed he'd shared with her. *How long ago was this? I mean, he could have just been experimenting, right?*

This is going on right now. And he's been experimenting, as you called it since he was about thirteen. He also has very violent sex. I know the two of you have as well, but it's nothing compared to what he does when he's pissed off. He's killed at least three people that I'm aware of since he's been doing this. Tears fell down Margie's cheeks, but she didn't wipe them away. What would be the point in telling this woman she was hurt by it all? *I know you killed Rebecca. What I want to know is, did he tell you to do it?*

Not in words so much, but he said it would pave the way for the two of us getting together. I have done this before. I'm sure you know that. She said she did. *You know a great deal about me and Peter. Why is he still out and about when I'm wasting away here in a dank jail cell?*

Because of you, he's not done anything wrong. She

thought about that and realized he'd said that to her before. *Yes, I'm aware of him telling you that you'd not go to prison if you were caught killing someone. That's not true — you know that, don't you?*

I'm not a child anymore, so I guess I would have to go now. Meadow told her even back then, she'd have gone to prison. *I'm a mess, aren't I?*

As she started thinking of all the fucking shit she'd put up with over the years, the way he'd dangled a carrot in front of her to get her to do things for him, Margie just wanted to kill herself. Rather than face serious jail time, she knew she would rather die.

Look. I'm going to make some changes to your ordeal there. But you need to do something for me. It will go a long way in figuring out for both of us what Peter's plans are for you. She said she wanted to get out. *Right now, that's not possible. Peter is pressing charges, and you did try and burn his home down. Think of it this way, Margie — you're safe where you are. No one can accuse you of any wrongdoing while you're there.*

What is it you want me to do? I'll do most anything to get things moving here. I never thought I'd say this, but I hate myself. I hate everything about me. Meadow didn't say anything for several moments, and she thought she'd left her. *Meadow?*

I'm here. I'm looking into things for a second here. All right. A cop is going to come to you to offer you a phone call. I want you to call Peter and ask him if he's going to bail you out of jail. All right? Margie asked her what was that going to do when she got out. *We'll cross that bridge when we get to it. If we do.*

You don't think he's going to do it, do you? No answer was telling her Meadow didn't think he would.

The officer showed up and asked her if she wanted to make a phone call. Telling him she did, she followed him down the hallway toward the little office to her right. Calling Peter, she heard him answer and started to cry. "Will you please come and bail me out of here? I don't like it. There isn't the kind of food that I like, and I'm sleeping on a cot that no telling how many people have slept in. Please?"

"No." She'd known on some level that was what he was going to say, but it still crushed something deep inside of her. "You tried to burn me out, Margie. I mean, what would I have done if you'd succeeded? No. I like you in jail. If I have a need for you, then I might consider it. But for now, you should think about your actions and what it would have done to the two of us had you been able to get things going to the point of no return."

"Can't you just use some of the money you have stashed away to get me out? I'll stay away until you need me." He started cursing, then asked her what sort of phone she was using. "The payphone. It says right here they're not recording anything on this device. Why do you ask?"

"I don't want anyone to know I have that money,

Margie. That's going to be my getting out of jail run money." She knew that too. That was why she'd lied to him. The laminated sign on the table where she was sitting specifically told her this phone would be recorded, and by using it with this knowledge, the user was agreeing to the terms of it being used against her. She asked him if she was going to be going with him. "Yes. Of course. Haven't you always been my best girl? I mean, whatever would I do if you didn't come with me? No, you just stay where you are, and I'll work on something on my end here. But in the meantime, you have to learn your place, Margie. You can't just burn my home down when I'm inside when you get into a snit. I'll talk to you in a couple of days. But I'd not expect anything different right now. You've got to learn to behave."

Putting the phone down, she sat there for several minutes just thinking about what he'd said to her. And also the things he'd not. Peter didn't want her anymore. Not only that but she only just realized that he was still treating her like that child she'd been when he'd taken her to his home. A child.

The door opened behind her, and she started to ask for a few more minutes. Instead, the officer that had brought her to this room laid a tray in front of her and told her she had an hour to eat. Taking the tin lid off the dinner plate, she cried at what was there—her favorites.

You will get one of these meals a day brought to you. Nothing that the other patrons are getting. Let me know if you'd rather have it for dinner or lunch. I can make arrangements to have bottled water brought to you as well. I'm sorry about what Peter is doing to you. It hadn't even occurred to her that Peter might have been the one that had sent it. Meadow was doing just what she had said she would.

Everything was still hot and very good. The steak was perfection, and the tiny mushrooms were done just the way she loved them. There was even a strawberry shortcake, just like she'd had as a child, with more strawberries than cake. The ice cream was still frozen, and she ate every bite of it. When she was finished, as full as she'd ever been, she was escorted back to her cell, where she not only found a stash of bottled water but a soft blanket as well as a pair of beautiful slippers to wear around. Crying and holding her bounty to her, she heard Meadow speak once again.

The things in your room are from your sister. I told her what happened to you with Peter, and she wanted you to know she was thinking about you. She asked her to thank her. *I will. She also said she'd like to help you. To get you some help. I think once this shit hits the fan, you're going to need all you can get. Will you cooperate with us?*

Yes. You've been true to your word so far, and I don't know why. But yes, you tell me what you want, and I'll make sure I do it for you. Meadow asked her if she knew the combination to the safe in Peter's basement. *I do, but it's a decoy. The only thing in it is a will that was his father's and some kind of codebook. I read it before I started writing up his notes in the one that Becky took from him.*

I'm sorry. What did you just say? She told her that since she'd been a child, she'd been putting things into the book that Peter told her to do. *Are there any more of them? Books, I mean?*

Yes. I have them. You can have them if you want. Anything to make sure that...do you think I'll have to serve much in the way of jail time? I know it's a given that I will serve some time, but the more I think about it, the more I think I've been manipulated. By a grown fucking gay man. Margie laughed. *Not that I care who he fucks when we're not together, but I'm finding I don't think I have ever liked him. Much less loved him.*

I'm glad to hear you say that, Margie. There might be hope for you yet. So long as you don't fuck this up for yourself by backtracking your ass back to Peter and telling him what you've been up to. If you do, then whatever happens to you in prison will seem like a leisurely bath compared to what I will do to you. Margie started to tell her she'd never do that, but she also knew Peter knew her better than anyone. She asked Meadow if she'd be there to help her along. *Yes. And that's a good sign as far as I'm concerned. Knowing that you can be manipulated is going to be very helpful for you in the long run. I'll help you as long as you do just what you're told to do.*

The two of them spoke throughout the night. She even got to talk to Joey for a little while. It was wonderful to hear her voice, she thought, and not hear the anger in it. Joey was going to come and see her tomorrow, but she wasn't to tell anyone. That was fine with Margie. She really did want to see her sister.

After the connection or whatever it was closed up, she thought about the things she knew about her mom and wondered if that would help too. Perhaps, she thought, but only if it was something that was hurting Joey. She didn't think it was just yet, but Margie decided to keep her ear to the ground where her mom was concerned. She'd have to have help with that, of course. Meadow had been so helpful with things that she thought for sure she'd be able to trust her with this thing. Closing her eyes, thankful that she was doing something productive for a change, Margie fell into a dreamless sleep.

Chapter 6

With so many ideas buzzing in her head, Joey almost didn't want to leave the new building she was working in. Harvey was working the phones for her today so she could work, and Cybill had come in to help out with getting things organized for her on the upper levels. It was wonderful starting fresh, she thought. And having more room than she'd ever dreamed of having. Turning when she heard her door open, she ran to Pierce and hugged him several times before she could speak.

"Isn't this wonderful? I have so much room I just don't know where to start." He let her drag him around the large building. "I even have a place to pack things up before I send them out. Look at this. Demi thought they'd be much nicer for people to receive if they were packaged up with tissue paper. Do you have any idea how long I've wanted to do that? And my mom? Well, she's had to go in the house for a minute. It was just too much new for her."

"This is perfect. I can see you working against that

wall over there. I did wonder if you'd want to block out the windows or not. But I can see now how helpful that would be, as people would be wearing their new things in the sunlight." He marveled with her at the nice cutting boards she had, even taking her to the area where she had lots of extras hanging. "Demi was asking me if I'd see about the dresses you designed. She said that she and Lucian have this thing, and she wanted to see if you had something she could wear. All you women are so tiny, I bet it makes it easy for you to swap things around."

He was so sweet, and she loved him for it. Dancing around the building, she pointed out things to him she'd only just discovered. When they ended up in the main part of the building again, she finally sat down when he asked her to. She was so giddy she had to sit on her hands while he spoke.

"I've finally gotten around to looking for the stuff Alan sent to us. There is a lot of it that I think we need to talk about." Joey asked him if it was bad. "None of it is bad. Just a great deal of cash, as well as property that will have to be dealt with. A lot. And Gaea gave us some old seeds I'm excited about planting."

"How much is a lot? By the way, I did go to the bank and put my name on all your accounts. Well, I signed my name to them. You have to do the same to mine that have been set up for us to share." He nodded, but she could tell he was very distracted. "Whatever it is, Pierce, you've already proven to me that we can make anything work so long as we're together. Just tell me. We'll deal with it together."

"I called Alan. He was laughing so hard it was pissing me off. I asked him how he'd been able to give us this chest. After telling me how old he was and how long he's been investing, I thought it was possible. So I called my brothers. We all have the same. Not that it would have mattered to any of us if one got more than the— Mom and Dad got a little more, I think, but that's all right. And of course, Lucy did get some extra for her part in—"

"Just say it." She was glad she was sitting down when he told her the number. "I'm sorry. Did you just tell me there is over a billion dollars in our house right now?"

"No." She smiled at him, glad for the mistake on her part. "There is over eight billion in our house right now. Not including the gems he put in there, as well the fact that we own a great deal of land. Land in places that—"

She put her hand up to stop him. "Are you sure? I mean, did you count it?" He told her there was a note on top of each of their trunks breaking down what was in it. "He actually gave each of you eight billion dollars? Christ, what did he do, rob banks his entire life?"

"He told me he owned a couple of diamond mines. We own one of them, and Lucian owns the other. There are also other mines that the others own. They're all high producing places too." She asked if that meant there would be more. "Yes. Lots, I guess. But that's not the point. What the hell are we going to do with that much money?"

"Spend it?" She shook her head and asked for a moment when he growled at her. "You've had more time to digest this, Pierce. I'm getting it all in one lump." He told her he was sorry. "What do your parents think of this?" He said he wasn't brave enough to ask them if they'd opened theirs yet. "Probably a good thing. I remember Cindy telling me how upset they were when Demi put money into their accounts when she came to be mated with Lucian. What on earth was he thinking? Do you think he had this just lying around his house all this time? I mean…well, not the property. That would be difficult to hide in a home, I guess."

"You're babbling." She told him to fuck off. "Yes, that's what I told Lucian when he started doing the same thing. Something about taxes on it would kill them. Putting them in a different tax bracket. I don't think there is a tax bracket for this much money."

"That's more than likely why it's all in cash." He seemed to understand that as soon as she said it. "I mean, he wouldn't have had to file a return. I think, from what I understand, Alan's well over the age limit of having to do that. I'm babbling again. I just— Pierce, we could buy anything and everything we've ever thought of. Not that I want to do that. That would be like announcing to the world we've come into a windfall." She giggled, then had to stop herself. "This is the strangest conversation I think I've ever had in all my life. What to do with too much money."

She leaned back in the chair, wanting just a moment to change the subject. "My sister wants to see me. I'm going to go there tomorrow and see what she wants. Also, I'm to understand that Meadow has been speaking to her. Do you have any idea what she might have been talking to her about?" He said he wasn't aware she had been. "I didn't think you would be. When the officer spoke to me, I asked him what she might want, and he told me he thought Margie had been doing a lot of thinking. Soul searching, I guess. And that she's made a few calls that have been recorded to Peter Hightower."

"I can see Meadow having her do that. Perhaps to see just what sort of person he is. But as I said, I don't know. Are you going alone? I can't go tomorrow. We have to get the paperwork finished up today, so I can go into one of the buildings in Columbus and put in new cameras. They're having a great deal of shortages." She thought she'd ask Meadow to go with her. "You should take them all. Even if it's a good meeting with Margie, they'd be willing to celebrate with you. If not, they'd be there to help you pick up the pieces."

"What do you think of my mom going?" He stared at her for several seconds before asking her why she'd be worried. "I don't know. I mean, she's told me everything.

I think. And I've been talking to Demi and Mel about the things going on with the video that surfaced. Blake whatshisname isn't paying any more to Peter either, I've been told."

"Do you think she's lying to you about the thing?" She shook her head, as sure about that as she was anything. "Then I don't see anything wrong with taking her if she wants to go. However, I'd ask Margie if she minds if she comes in to talk to her. If she really is doing some soul searching, as you think, you don't want to hurt your chances of getting her to help you get Peter out of the picture for good, do you?"

"To be honest with you, I don't know what to think. She's been this person I don't like for so long I find it hard to believe she would ever be able to change." Pierce said he could understand that. "I'm going. I don't have any problem with going to see what she wants, but I'm not sure what good it will do either of us."

"Then you shouldn't go." Joey asked him why not. "Because you've already decided whatever she has to say to you isn't going to matter, right? If you don't want to go and have an open mind, too, then there isn't any point in you going to hear what she might have to say. For all you know, it could be that she doesn't want to see you again. And with the way you're thinking, that would be all right with you. However, if she wants, after all this time, to make amends, then I'd say going there with a closed mind will do neither of you any good. But that's just me.

About this money. I think we should perhaps just leave it where it is for now and use it when something comes up we want to be a part of. I don't know what that would be, but it would be nice to have in the event an emergency comes up."

"What sort of emergency do you figure is going to cost eight billion dollars?" They were both laughing when he left her there to get to work, and she sat in her chair thinking about what he'd said to her. "I hate it when he's right."

It was nearly one when Cybill said she was going to the bakery. The kid was working hard here—she wondered how she wasn't exhausted before going to her other job. But it was nice having someone helping her. There wasn't any way she'd be able to get this up and running all on her own. Having the help was nice.

Harvey joined her for a late lunch. She'd ordered sandwiches from the Gathering Place.

"There are any number of people wanting to know if you're going to be hiring. I've been telling them that for now, you're just setting the place up. I'm to understand you're going to be working with two other businesses in town in opening up a shipping store. That would be just the ticket, I'm thinking. Getting things sent out in a timely manner would be making you some happy customers." They talked about the pretty way things were going to be shipped out. "I like that idea. When my missus used to order things from a couple of places, she'd get so frustrated with them when they'd just jammed something in a box and slapped a label on it. She'd tell me it would only take a couple of minutes for someone to put a pretty bow on the product or even to put in a nice little thank you card. She didn't even mind that it was manufactured. She just liked the thought that went into putting it together."

"Mel said that putting a coupon code in the box wasn't all that good either. People would want coupons before they ordered. I'm not sure how I can make that work just now, but I'm thinking on it. She's right, however. I don't know how many of those things I put up to use later and would either forget where I stuck them, or they'd be expired when I went to use them."

Harvey had a lot of good ideas to go along with shipping. His wife must have loved online shopping. "No, not so much online, but there used to be a lot of those television shows that would sell stuff to the public. She'd get on there once in a while and talk to the host doing the show. Some of the things she got made really nice gifts when we needed one in a hurry. Other times they'd just sit in the corner and draw up some dust bunnies." He laughed a little, and it sounded so sad to her. "When she passed on, I found boxes of things she'd ordered that hadn't been taken out of the box yet. She had it in her head, I guess, who it was to go to. There were little post-it notes all over things. I gave away those that I could and donated the rest of it. She was a good woman, my

Milly. Didn't spend too much, but she sure did like to give things away. I think she made herself a good bit of friends by doing that. Sure did make her happy."

"That's all that mattered to you, isn't it, Harvey?" He nodded as he gathered up the papers his sandwich had come in. "Harvey, I have a question for you."

After telling him what Pierce had said about Margie and for Joey to have an open mind, Harvey stayed seated as he seemed to be thinking on what she'd asked him. If she was going in there closed minded or not.

"You already know the answer, don't you?" She didn't want to admit she did but did tell him she was afraid Pierce was right. "There you go. You've admitted you're afraid you're going to close off your mind. So why subject yourself to all her negativity?" He stood up. "But, what if you're wrong on all this? What if, after spending some time in a jail cell—which ain't no place for a lady, I don't think—she has had some time to think things over? What would you do right now if you knew if you didn't go see her, she'd be dead tomorrow? All these things here, those are things you have to think about when you talk to a loved one. Because I'm betting no matter how dirty she treated you, you still love your sister."

Joey watched his struggle with telling her that. As she watched tears roll down his weathered cheeks, something occurred to her about this man. He was hurting. Hurting deeply into his heart that very few ever knew about.

"I do. Your wife, Milly — you had a fight before she passed, didn't you?" He nodded. "She loved you too, Harvey. No matter the spats that you might have had, I'm betting she not only forgot about how upset she was with you but that she also kissed you on the forehead and told you how much she loved you."

He had a small burst of laughter before nodding. "She did at that. But with a little pop to the back of the head too. She didn't want me to think I'd gotten too much by her." He laughed a little longer this time like he'd forgotten how to laugh. "She was a pistol, my Milly. You're like her, so you know. That's why I wanted to work with you here. I have nothing back home to hold me there but some memories. Good ones, but too many for an old man like me to be around all the time. I like it here too. I got me a few friends that I have something to eat with in the morning. A good meal to take home with me. Milly, she'd be fussing at me about having food brought in, but she'd not mind too much knowing I'm having a good meal. Yes, sir. You're a good deal like her." He started to leave, then turned back to her. "If you don't go and see her, Joey, you're going to kick your bottom for a long time. What does it take for you to mosey on over there, have a talk with her, and come home? For all you know, it could be the best thing that ever happened to either of you. It certainly can't hurt."

She was going to do it. And in some way, she hoped, make some kind of headway into learning more about

Margie. They were sisters. Not close, but sisters. Surely, after all this time, she could get to know something about her. Something good. Tomorrow morning she was going to do it, damn it. And she was going to make sure Margie didn't need anything.

~*~

Peter didn't know what to think about Margie and her calling him all the time. Damn it, did she think he didn't have anything to do but to talk to her about coming down there to bail her out? He liked her there for the sole reason that he didn't have to perform sexually for her. It had been getting harder and harder for him to even think about seeing her naked in front of him, she was so revolting to him. Not her, he supposed, but the things she'd require of him. Fucking her had become something of a nightmare.

She'd been his go to person when he needed something, and now all he had was this idiot that didn't know shit. However, he was about the best looking idiot he'd ever met. But that wasn't going to color his mood in killing him if he didn't get his shit together.

"What do you mean, you can't find Blake Daniels? I all but took you to his home to get him to pay what he owes me. I told you before you left, if he didn't pay, you were to beat the shit out of him until he did." He told him the house was empty. "Empty? Of him or everything?"

"There is nothing in the house but this here letter. It's addressed to you. But there isn't even a paper towel in the kitchen I could use to pick it up." He didn't bother asking him about why he'd need that to pick up an envelope. He'd already discovered the man was a germophobe. Not with everything, but enough to make Peter nuts with it. "I didn't read it."

He put the envelope on his desk and told the kid to go away. Not that Peter tried to remember his name, but if all else failed on that, kid worked every time. He knew that not only would Margie have known his name, but she would also have known everything there was to know about him.

As soon as the door closed behind the kid, Peter tore into the envelope. Dumping the contents on the desk, always fearful of someone sending him some poison—a trick he'd pulled a few times—Peter looked at the penny stuck to a piece of cardboard. No note. Nothing to explain what it was supposed to mean. Turning it over, he looked at the phone number on the back.

He had emergency phones for things like this. Hell, he even had some stock in one of the many companies that manufactured them. Pulling out one from his desk drawer, he was glad to see it had been charged up and was ready for him to use. Almost as soon as he finished putting in the phone number, a woman answered.

"Hello, dumbass." He asked her who she was. "I don't think I'll give you that right now. But I did want to tell you why you're calling me. There will be no more payments to you from either Blake Daniels or Lauren

Mathews. That ship has sailed. Also, you'll be thrilled to know that I've taken back all the money they've paid you and given it to them. We both know the video wasn't real."

"What the hell do you mean, you've taken the money back? You can't do that." He turned on his computer to see where she might have gotten the money from. The one account in the bank not far from where he lived had over seven thousand dollars in it. However, almost as soon as he clicked on it to see transactions, the account was at a zero balance. Terrified now, he looked at all his accounts, even the ones he had overseas. They all looked good, so he closed up the accounts and leaned back in his chair. "I see you think you got the better of me in emptying my bank account. There is insurance for those sorts of things, so I'm not worried."

"Then you'd better have a look at your two accounts in the Cayman Islands again. I do believe they're empty as of now too. Oh, and insurance doesn't cover those accounts. Since you didn't gain the money legally, you have no legal standing in having it put back." Opening the accounts again, he saw they were indeed emptied. Not only were they empty, but she'd not even left a penny in the accounts to keep them open. "That's why we sent you a penny, Hightower. So you could put it into your account to keep it open. However, I don't know how that will work on your end. Again, it was obtained illegally."

Her laugh hurt his head. It was as if it were pinging

off the inside of his skull in a way that made him sick with it. Turning off his computer, rebooting it to see if he was just being played with, he found that the accounts were not closed. That if he had a question about it, there was a number for him to call.

"Why are you doing this to me? I don't know you from Adam. Put my money back, and I'll forget this ever happened. I'll even stop hounding Blake and Lauren for the money. How's that?" She just laughed again. "Look, bitch. Put that money back or so help me, I'm going to hunt you down and tear you a new ass."

"I have it on good authority, Peter, that you're going to prison. For a very long time." He asked her on what charges. "Anything and everything in your little book of information. It was wonderful of you to have had someone I could speak to who kept track of things for you. You'd not believe how helpful people have been when we've gone to their back yards to look for the bodies."

"Becky? That kid doesn't know her ass from a hole in the ground. She stole that from me, thinking it was important. It's not. Not the least bit." It was, and he was sure she knew it. "Whatever you think you have, young lady, you don't have shit. Just give it back to me, and we'll call it even. Of course, after you put my money back. I will have it by the end of the day."

"You go on thinking you can make me do anything." She hummed a little bit, and he thought he knew the tune, but she spoke before he could get a good hold on it. "By the way, I want to thank you for all the money you've donated to several good causes. I won't tell you which ones—I'm thinking you'll try and get it back from them before they've had a chance to use it. However, it is going to help a great many families out this year."

"Why are you doing this to me? I don't know you. You obviously don't know me, or you'd know better than to fuck with me." She said she knew who he was and that he was powerless to touch her. "You think so, do you? I have the long arm of the law in my pocket. They'll do what I tell them, or they'll be in worse trouble than you are right now."

"How do you suppose that is going to work? You have no idea who I am. You don't know where I'm living. Nor what I am. And I'm a what, not a who." Peter asked her what that was supposed to mean. "Well, for one thing, I can be in and out of places in a flash without you ever seeing me. Like, right now, I know you have twenty-three burner phones in your desk drawer. On the top of it is a picture of your late mother. She wasn't a good person either, was she, when she found out you liked to dick little boys instead of a nice woman? Of course, you blamed it on her, but that never flew either, did it? Also, you have an engraved pen set there from someone named Margie. Was she—? I started to ask you if she was your lover, but that's not right, is it? She and you, the different parts of each of you, would have turned you off."

"You think you know so much. You fucking bitch. I'm going to find you if it's the last thing I do." She told him she hated that saying. "Why? I'm guessing you have a good reason for not wanting me to hunt you down? I don't care."

"No. It's not that. You can hunt for me all you want, but you said you were going to find me if it was the last thing you did. Why would you continue looking for me if you've already found me? I mean, that would be just nuts for you to keep on looking after you've found me. Don't you agree?" He had no idea what she was talking about. "Never mind. It must be too much over your head for you to understand even a little fun. Also, you'll be glad to know your home is being taken for back taxes. I don't know how you think you were so special that you didn't have to file them, but you should be getting a knock at your door right about now." The doorbell sounded, and he heard the kid say he had it. "That kid. He's a nice kid, don't you think? His name is Jimmy, by the way. He works for me too. That's why he's not doing what you want him to."

"What do you mean, he works for you? He's getting paid by me." She said he'd better check on that. Jimmy had been there for nine days now, and no one had paid him shit. "I guess I won't be able to either since you took all my money from me. What the hell do you want?"

"Mr. Hightower? My name is Agent Skinner. I'm here with the Internal Revenue Service. We need to have a long talk with you about the nonpayment of taxes and such. We've been notified that you have been cheating the United States government of some tax money." He told him he didn't know what he was talking about. "Well, then you'll have proof of your reasons, I'm guessing. If you'd like to come with me—or not. It matters little to us at the IRS what you want to do. But we're going to need all your records, as well as any receipts you have on things for this place and the other four we've found that you have your name on."

"Again, I have no idea what you're referring to. I have a girlfriend that has a couple of homes, but they're not mine." He hoped to Christ Margie had never found out about the shit that was in her name. She could easily own his ass. "This house is hers too, I think. We did that in the event something were to happen to me, she'd be set up. I'm a much older man than she is."

So Margie is wealthy? The voice in his head had him looking around for her. He asked her where she was. *Not out there where anyone can see me. I'm going to have to dig a little deeper into this. She should be getting compensated for fucking you.*

"Do you hear that? There is a woman speaking to me. She called me earlier, and now she's talking to me." The man, Agent Skinner, said they were the only two in the room. "I know that, you moron. I can see we're the only two in here. But she's speaking to me right now. Telling me she's going to be investigating why Margie's name is on things and not mine. She's going to cause me trouble. That woman already took all my money."

"You have money, do you? Not according to your records, you don't." Agent Skinner sat down in the chair. "Why don't you tell me what she's saying to you, and we'll work from there. How about that?"

It was then it occurred to him that he had better keep his mouth shut. It didn't help him at all that whoever was speaking to him was taunting him. Telling him she'd found four houses so far, including the one he was living in. He tasted blood. He was trying so hard to keep his mouth shut. When he found her, he was going to shut her up in the most permanent way.

"Nothing?" He shook his head. "Oh well. I guess it was too good to be true about her helping a man out." She egged him on, telling him to call the man a moron again. She was sure, she told him, that would go over very well. "Come on then. You tell us where you've got your receipts and such, and we'll get this taken care of. Whoever this Margie is, she should have someone clean up in here. I think it smells like someone is going to jail."

Skinner was laughing as he stood there waiting on him to get things gathered up. There wasn't any way he was going to try and find things to take with him. Hell, he didn't have the first clue as to where things were. Everything that he owned was in Margie's name. Hopefully, that would count for something. However, not with the luck he was having right now. Things were going to shit, and he was going to be the plunger to make it go down easier for everyone involved.

I'm going to have to have a long talk with Margie. I'm betting she thinks she's fucked. Well, isn't it going to be just wonderful for her to find out that not only does she have a place to live, but enough money to have a nice life? Without you. He asked her if she'd go and get Margie out of jail. *Nope. I think she's a tad bit safer there than out with you. Oh boy, is this going to be great. You have yourself a nice time with the Feds, Peter. This will teach you to fuck with people's minds.*

Chapter 7

Joey watched the people coming and going into the jail. There had been some talk about someone being really sick. She found out just now that it wasn't her sister. She didn't know why, but it worried her on so many levels that Peter might well try and harm Margie for what she knew about him. At this point, Joey didn't dismiss anything the man would do to get what he wanted.

"She's looking better." Joey turned when Meadow spoke to her as her sister was being brought through the door. Margie did look better. Not only was her hair pulled back from her face, but she looked years younger than she normally did. "Must be from having someone take her seriously."

"I'm betting when she hears about Peter, she's going to have a fit." As soon as she was unchained, Margie hugged her. It was brief and not allowed, but it felt as if she'd put everything she had wanted to share with her in that simple touch. "You look wonderful."

She said it before she could think about how Margie

would take it. Instead of getting upset as she usually did, asking her if she had looked horrible before this, Margie thanked her. Sincerely too, it seemed to her. Then when she was allowed to, Joey reached out and put her hand over Margie's.

"How are you doing?" Margie had to turn away for a moment, and Joey let her. The tears were right there where she could see them, and she wanted to hug her again. "I've been making sure you're getting extra things. I hope they're all right for you. I realized I knew very little about you after all these years."

"I know no more about you than I could get from one of your people. I'm so sorry about that. I've been thinking about so much while in here. I have a lot of time." Margie looked at Meadow. "You look nothing like I thought you would. I mean, I've imagined all sorts of ugliness when we first started talking. Then as you began to help me, I still didn't get it right. Thank you so much, Meadow. I wouldn't have survived without you there most of the time."

"You deserve better than Peter. Hell, anyone deserves better than Peter." Waiting for the outburst with Margie defending Peter, it startled Joey when it never came. Her sister had never let anyone bad mouth Peter since she was only a child. "Your sister is here to visit you. I only came by to give you this. I've spoken to Joey, and she can answer any questions you might have. If not, you both know how to reach me."

The file was put on the table, and Meadow got up. Joey looked at her sister again. Wondering if they'd be all right alone made her nervous. But as soon as Margie smiled at her, things in her mind and heart settled down considerably.

"I didn't think you'd come to see me. Not that I can blame you for not wanting to come here. Who wants to be in a jail on a nice cold day? I'm glad you did." Margie pulled the file toward her, and Joey thought about how she really didn't know Margie at all. "Where did you get this?"

The picture was a still of the video that Mom had, the one Peter had been blackmailing her with. After telling her sister what it was and who she thought the other two men were, Margie shook her head. Asking for and getting a box of tissues, she cried for a few minutes before she spoke to her again.

"This is me, not Mom. That's not Blake either. Blake is much taller than this man. Is this what he'd been telling her he was going to release to ruin you?" Joey told her that was what she'd heard from both Mom and Blake. "Peter did this to her. And to you. I had no idea when he made me do this that was his intention. He told me he wanted to have this done so that when I moved on to greener pastures, he could look back on it and— You know, more and more every day I realize how he played me. Not just for things like this, but everything in my life has been one lie after the other. Did you know that he's a homosexual? I didn't. I thought he was just too old. Or he'd blame whatever kind of issues we were having on me. My unwillingness to conform, he said."

"Conform to who? Him? I believe you're much too strong willed to conform to anything you don't want to." Margie thanked her. "I don't think that came out right. I meant it to make you realize how much smarter than him you are."

"I'm beginning to see that too. And I didn't take it the wrong way." She looked at the file again. "I want, if it's possible, to be friends at least. I've fucked up a lot. I know that now. I've never been a nice person. Not to you, not to Mom, or to anyone that wasn't Peter. And all he did was run me into the earth by having me keep pushing and pushing you guys away. I don't even understand why he cared so much if you were successful or not."

"I don't know either. It would be something he might only have in his head." She pulled the file to her. "Meadow can get into his mind and found out some things that are going to benefit you. Everything he owns is in your name. Bank accounts. Homes. Stocks and bonds. She has moved all the overseas money to a couple of banks here in the States for you to use."

Putting her hand over hers, Margie looked at her sister. "You didn't have to do any of this. You didn't have to do a lot of things I know you're doing for me. I get a good meal when I ask for it. Not that they're bad here, but I'm eating better than I think I ever did. There are extra blankets when I need them. It's the little things, I've discovered, that can make a night alone locked up so much easier to deal with. I would be here alone, without shit, except for your help. I've burnt so many bridges, Joey, that I'm—"

"Don't. You're my sister, Margie, and you always will be. I will tell you that there are times, even sitting here today, that I'm afraid of what you're going to say to me. Do to me. But I'm working through them. I love you." Margie told her she loved her very much. "When we get all this settled about Peter, you will come and stay with us, and we'll have a wonderful time."

"I'd like that. Very much, I think." They went over each of the pages in the file. Margie was given permission to take notes and to be able to keep them. Also, Joey gave the primer to her with the coded book that Becky had gotten. "Meadow said you have something for me to sign about Rebecca. My confession."

"Yes." Handing her one of the papers at the bottom of the file, she watched her sister read over it. "We're going to have a private service for her tomorrow. Nothing in the paper. I think with everything going on, it would be better for everyone if we were to just pretend like we knew nothing about her being killed."

"You know who did it, right?" She nodded. "I thought I was doing the right thing with that. I've been warned not to say anything that can be recorded, but I wanted you to know I'm so very sorry I was involved."

They spent the rest of their time going over all the paperwork that was going to be needed for the transfer of the property to her name. Alan told her that if everything was signed over to Joey, she could use it for Margie's legal defense. There would be a trial, he told her, and with her sister cooperating like this, it would look good for her to be getting some serious time cut off her sentence.

"Alan Shoe is going to be working with an attorney to help with your case. He wants you to know he's going to work for a manipulation case for you. Telling the jury you were much too young when things started out for the two of you and that he should have known better." Margie said she should have too. "Perhaps. But we'd only just lost Dad, and Mom was really out of it. I think under the circumstances, you did what you thought you needed to in order to get by. But he took it too far."

"There were times when he'd just show up at school and take me places. Wild and wonderful places that only a child would think that way about. Bars and the tracks. I think I spent more time at the tracks with a bunch of drunks than I did in school." She smiled at her then. "I'm working on getting my education while I'm in here. Not much right now, as I've only just started, but I'm going to make sure I work on it when I'm out. I've missed out on so many things."

"Just don't get frustrated and stop."

Margie said, "Yes, Mother."

"You know what I mean. I don't know that I could start over like that. I would do it, but it would be difficult. But luckily you don't have to worry about working while you're doing this. And you've got family around."

"I hope I still have family around after everything comes out." Patting her hand again, Joey told her she would. "I guess you've met someone. Meadow told me you have a nice man in your life, as well as his entire family. She was telling me about her magic too. I don't want to die in here alone, Joey."

Holding her while she sobbed about what sort of person she'd become, Joey just kept telling her over and over how much she was going to be able to do once she was over this thing with Peter. How he'd been hurting her for years, and now that he was going to prison, she could move on. Joey expected at any time for someone to come and tell them to break it up. But no one did, not even bothering with her time limit when it came and went. Reaching out to Meadow, she asked her what was going on.

You must be doing it. I mean, I don't know why not. She said she wasn't magical. That was why not. *Nope, you are. Just as the rest of the family is. Remember standing in the room when the magic was dispersed?*

I wasn't aware of any changes that occurred to me. Meadow just laughed. *I don't think I like you very much. You're a very rude woman.*

I am at that, and you know you love me. I'm adorable.

I've not heard myself called that, but I think it works. I've been working on some things in here while I'm wandering around. This place is shitty. Joey told her that was why it was jail. It wasn't supposed to be five star. *It should at least have some working showers. There are seventeen people in this place that depend on things working for them. There is one shower. People are reduced to taking one shower a week, so they don't overload the hot water heater. And there are rooms with space heaters right outside the cells that try to keep them warm. I'm thinking that as a family, we can help this place out a little bit.*

Yes, I agree. Why don't we call it the Peter Hightower Jail? That'll be just what he deserves.

They both laughed, and Meadow said she'd work on that. Joey told Margie when she was better what she and Meadow had been talking about. She laughed about calling it the Hightower Jail.

"I might have to look into this." Joey asked her if she was serious. "I don't know. I want to make a difference. I know you are with your new family. I guess I've been sucking on the tit of society long enough, don't you think?"

"I think I love this new person you're becoming."

They visited after all the paperwork was gone over, making sure the places where Margie was supposed to sign were all in place as she shoved them back into the file. The picture was the only thing that remained on the table between them. The file was now in her purse.

"I don't remember this guy's name, but the rest I

do. I'll write them on here for you to contact. If you need them." Joey told her that at this point, she had no idea what she might need or not. "Me either. I should have been an attorney instead of a whore, I guess."

"Don't say that. That's not true." Margie told her it was exactly true. She'd become a bed partner to a man that paid her to have sex with him. "Okay, I suppose that is the definition, but don't say that about yourself again. You're not the same person you were. All right?"

"Yes, all right." After writing down the names of the people on the photo, she even wrote down who the camera man was, as well as anyone else that was in the room when it happened. "I was wondering if I should have told you about Mom being blackmailed. Peter didn't tell me what she'd done, or anything like that, other than it was really terrible and that you would hate her forever for it. I guess he thought we looked enough alike that no one would question it. I don't want to even think about what he would have done to get me to say it was her all the time. But that's over with, and I want to think I'm stronger for what he did to me. I'm certainly feeling a good deal smarter for it."

"Lesson learned, right?" Margie agreed with her, and they talked again. This time about nothing to do with Peter or her sister's relationship with him. "You should see our house, Margie. It's huge and so nicely laid out. You'll love it there."

"I will love it anywhere that's not here." They

laughed, and that was when she noticed that her sister had been yawning. She asked her if she was tired. "I am. I mean, sitting around makes for a lazy day. They get us up so early here that I'm usually in bed by nine or nine-thirty."

"I'll let you go." Margie asked if she'd be back. "I will. Tell Meadow what you might need from me, and I'll make sure I bring it to you. Anything you need, all right?"

"I've got most of what I need in knowing you're going to come back." Something entered her head, a small thought, and Joey dismissed it before it could grow. "I'll be seeing you soon, right Joey?"

"Yes. Very soon. I'll come back in a couple of days with some more clothing for you too. They said you could have some underthings, and now that I've gotten your sizes, I'll bring you some."

She moved quickly out of the area after her sister was taken back. Meeting Meadow in the hall, she could tell that the other woman was upset. She only hoped it wasn't at her. Meadow told her that it wasn't before she could ask.

"Good. I have enough on my mind without thinking what kind of horrors you could think up about me."

"You'd survive them. You don't have much in the way of skeletons in your closet." That disturbed her on levels she didn't understand. "Don't worry about it, Joey.

If I ever have to take you out, I'll make sure it's quick."

Staring at the other woman while she had a good laugh at her expense, she wondered how much of the story was true as to what she'd done with her own tormentor. All of it, she'd bet now. And perhaps even more that people might not want to know about. No, right then, Joey knew she was going to stay on the best side of all the McCray women. Especially this one. She had powers that would turn a man's hair white in a matter of seconds.

~*~

Pierce listened to Joey talking about her visit and her thoughts that kept circling around in her head. Her sister, she told him, had learned from the best about manipulating someone, and she was afraid she was just good enough to slip by all of them to get what she wanted.

"Did you talk to Meadow about it?" She shook her head, and he wondered aloud why she'd not. "If anyone can see what's in a person's head, it would be her, I believe. You should really do it before it drives you crazy."

"I don't know. Isn't that sort of like telling her she's not right? I'm terrified of her if you want the truth. I think she's the scariest person alive." Pierce thought she was right but told her that she'd not hurt her. "Yeah, so she told me. If she had to ever kill me, she'd make it quick."

That got him laughing so hard that Joey slapped him. Telling him it wasn't funny only made him laugh all the harder. Finally, when he thought he could contain himself, he told her he was going to call Meadow over, and she was going to tell her what she thought.

"All right, but if I suddenly disappear, it's going to be on your head."

Meadow said she was in town and would be over soon. He didn't tell her what was going on. This was going to have to be from Joey. He had a feeling Meadow had been kidding with her, but he just wasn't sure anymore. The woman was the scariest person he'd ever met.

By the time Meadow showed up, Joey had worked herself up into a frenzy. She would sit for a few minutes, then get her tablet and start on a design. After a while, he thought about having her tied down so she'd relax, but he was slightly afraid of her too. He'd never seen anyone like this before.

"Don't hurt me." Meadow sat down across from Joey and then turned to him. When Meadow asked him to leave them alone, he went to the kitchen with his brother. Telling Josiah what was going on, he felt better when he said he'd not thought of that. How Margie could be just as bad, if not worse than Peter.

"I'll feel a good deal better when this is over." Josiah told him what had happened with the IRS. "They actually put him in jail? Great. One less thing we have to worry about concerning him. I mean, I guess he could still cause some hurt on Joey, or even Becky if he were to know where they are."

"Have you given any thought as to what you're going to do with your money? Meadow and I were talking about the jailhouse when you called her. I think there is more wrong with the place than there is working. And with Mel working with us on the security systems, I think it will be a good deal more secure too." Josiah told him the things Meadow had found when she'd been walking around. "I looked it up. There haven't been any renovations on the jail since the late sixties. And even then, it was only to put in extra phone lines. I know for a fact that the Internet isn't all that secure. I've been able to punch into the system whenever I need information without any trouble. Meadow said they share passwords too."

"A couple of weeks ago I had to drop off some camera equipment that had been stored in one of their buildings. Not one of them knew if the storage room had a camera on it all the time. I would think that would be the first place they'd put a camera." Josiah told him he would have thought the same thing. "I'm going to talk to the mayor about it. I think he's up for re-election, so he might want to play ball in order to get the votes he'll need. You should run."

"For what?" Pierce told him, laughing while he did so. "I don't want to be mayor. Christ, I don't have time to do the things I need to do as it is. I'm agreeing with you that someone else should take the job, but not me. I wouldn't know the first thing about it."

"Apparently, neither does the one in office now." Pierce handed him a flyer and waited while he read it over. "This is all over town. At the very least, he could have asked me to do it for him. Secondly, there are three misspelled words in the sucker."

"Four." He pointed to the fourth one. "All right, so he can't spell or put together a sentence. Why do you think he's doing such a shitty job? I mean, other than the camera thing, and that's mostly on the head of the person in the jail system, not so much him."

The paper, a flyer, said there was going to be a *Christmast* lite showing at the Count House. It gave the time and the day of the week, but a quick look at the calendar made him realize the mayor had the date incorrect as well. The Saturday he was referring to was actually a Wednesday. That would surely screw people up.

Another sheet of paper was handed to Pierce. This one, he had to sit down to read. It not only had misspelled words on it but was an invoice that asked for the *chef* of police to sign off on the paperwork for the new camera equipment that had been installed. He asked his brother if the address on the invoice was the mayor's office.

"Worse. It's his home address." Josiah went to his refrigerator and got them both a glass of tea while he explained. "I went by there, and it's all right there.

There is a state-of-the-art system in the back yard of his home, as well as over the front door. He can see who is coming on his cell phone from anywhere he has Internet service. Also, and this one really pissed me off, he's got himself a brand new car. I thought at the last meeting he was telling us he wasn't making it on the salary we were paying him, and he'd have to think about raising taxes so he could afford his bills."

The two of them were deep into looking into things when both Meadow and Joey joined them. Asking a few questions of Meadow, they were able to get information on quite a few things that were out of whack. Mostly it was things the city and county were paying for that were going into the personal residence of the mayor. She even suggested that their mom run for mayor.

"She'd do a fantastic job. And there isn't anything she'd want that she couldn't just go out and buy for herself." There was that, she agreed with Pierce. "Also, I think she'd get more of the beautification projects done, and under cost too. The very fact that we have to get permission from the moron to decorate for the holidays is simply stupid. That means the new Christmas shop can't decorate the outside of their shop until he says so. The thing is a fucking Christmas shop. The very name suggests it should be decorated with festive things all the time."

"You get to ask her about it?" Pierce asked Meadow why he had to ask. "Because I said so. And I like your wife. She is one smart cookie."

"Is she right?" Meadow nodded, looking so sad that it hurt him for both of them. "What did you find out? Other than the fact that she's playing her sister."

"That she's going to burn in hell for the things she's done to people." He didn't ask. Pierce wanted to know what that could be, but he wasn't sure he wanted to know exactly why they thought burning in hell was going to be something she would need. "She's been killing for him since she was just a child. Luring people into her little web of lies and then killing them while Peter watched. He might not like her overly much at the moment, but he certainly has her turning out to be just like him."

"I fell for it too easily." Josiah told Joey she'd not fallen for anything. "I know, but I could have. Easily. Who wants to know their sister is a monster like the one you're trying to keep her from? No one, that's who. But when Meadow dug really deep, she allowed me to look as well. The shit she has going on in her head is fucking scary. And how much she thinks killing me is going to be an easy time. I got news for her. I'm not the sap she thinks I am."

"But she has to play along with her. All the way up until we get her in court." Pierce asked why. "Because we want her to believe, throughout all of this, that she's pulled the wool over our eyes and that we're going to give her whatever she wants. I also had a chance to look into her head about signing over the money to Joey. She didn't care so long as Joey dies, and she gets it later rather than now. And that is her plan. To take not only what she has from Peter, but her sister as well."

Pierce asked Joey if she was all right. He knew she wasn't, not even close, but she did seem a great deal less stressed about it. It had to hurt her, he knew, to know her sister was this evil, diabolical person. He pulled her into his embrace as Josiah and Meadow argued about who was going to talk to his mom about running for the mayor seat. Then they had to convince their dad that he couldn't do it.

"He'll never get anything done. He'd be all over the town, that's for sure, but he'd be talking to everyone and anyone about who knows what before he remembered he should have been writing things down so he could take care of them. Last weekend Mom sent him to the store to pick up some flour. He was gone for nearly three hours and didn't come home with the flour. I think she expected that to happen and was glad for the few hours of quiet time." He laughed with the rest of them before going on about Dad going to the high school to have a look around. "The foreman had to call Demi to come and get him. Dad was out there on the beams looking at the jobs that were being done. If he had fallen, there is no telling what he might have done to himself. I love him to pieces, but he does need to think about what he does."

"Yes, that's for sure."

They ended up talking about going to dinner,

just the four of them. Inviting their parents was a great idea until they found out that Demi and Lucian were there too. Inviting everyone to the outing, Josiah told the others what the plan was and that they needed to convince Mom to run.

"Dad will help her. There isn't any doubt about that." He knew this too and was happy that Joey didn't seem to be as upset as she'd been before. "They're such a perfect couple. Don't you think? She puts up with him as much as he puts up with her. When he messes up, he knows it and goes to get her something to make up for it. I really think he does some of the things he does just to get her something. He told me that getting to see her face when he gets the right thing is well worth having her fuss at him for a little while."

"I don't think Dad has ever messed up in getting Mom the right thing." Josiah agreed with him. "Even when he really screws up, which isn't as often as he professes, he makes Mom smile when he shows up with a dozen roses or even a box of her favorite candy. You're right, Joey. They are the perfect couple."

On the way to dinner, Josiah said everyone agreed that Mom would make a great mayor. Presenting it to her was going to be tricky, they thought. They couldn't just tell her they thought she'd do a better job than the one they had now, then point out the things around town that she'd be able to fix up. The flowers were the biggest thing Mom didn't like. No flowers were planted outside in the urns the town had bought several years ago unless it was something approved for the entire town. Also, all the flowers had to be the same size and colors. So if one person didn't want to plant flowers, no one could. That really was a stupid thing, Pierce thought.

After everyone was settled into their seats, Demi and Lucian running behind because of little Alden, Pierce could tell that Mom was upset about something. When he asked her, she told him it would be fine. Then he asked her again.

"That mayor." Everyone quieted down and looked in her direction. "I've been talking it over with your father, and I'm going to run against him. Do you know he actually told me that my home was too new and that I wasn't to pretty it up too much so his home would look better? I had a mind to knock his head three ways from Sunday. Dad is going to help me and— What are you all laughing about?"

"Nothing, Mom. I think we were just picturing you hitting the mayor. You'd win. You know that, don't you?" She told him, of course, she would. "I knew it. You're going to be perfect for the job. And don't let any of these idiots here tell you anything different."

The rest of the dinner was just like that, having fun at others' expense as well as love and laughter all around. He loved these guys and would until his last breath. Which didn't look like it was going to happen for a very long time.

Chapter 8

The phone ringing pulled her from a deep sleep. Or was it just the beginning of her sleep? Whatever it was, Gabby was as pissed as she'd ever been at being woken up. Pulling the cell to her ear, she took a deep breath to blast the person on the other end when he spoke to her.

"Gabby, there's been an incident." She sat up in bed, untangling her hair from her face as she asked the officer what had happened. "Hailey is hurt. Badly. She's been beaten to shit, and the guy she was with is dead."

"I'm on my way. Did you call her dad?" Paul told her she'd asked for her. "All right. Paul, send a car for her dad in about five minutes. That'll give me— Where is she anyway?"

"Shanks farm. Right along the road. It's bad, Gabby. The kid looks like she's gone a few rounds with a fighter. But she's hanging on." She got outside and into her truck just as she saw an ambulance race by her home. "I'm going to tell her you're coming. All right. Hurry. I don't rightly think she's going to die right now, but I just don't know how she's still hanging onto consciousness as bad as she looks."

"I'm leaving my house now. I'll be there before you know it. Send someone for Harry. Don't tell him the way you have me. And for the love of all that is holy, don't let him drive."

She was pulling up in front of the cruisers that were all over the road. Gabby only had to show her badge to one person, and she was let through. Whoever the guy was, she didn't know him. More than likely, she thought, one of the guys from the county over. Going to the car, she had to look for her niece. Hailey was sitting on the ground leaning against the car, a bloodied, broken mess of a seventeen year old kid.

"Hey, babe. Isn't it a little cold for you to be sitting in the cornfield like this?" Hailey asked her if it was her. "Yes, honey, it's me. The medics are here to take you in. You look like hell." Her eyes were swollen shut, and it looked like her nose had been broken too. With her eye hanging oddly, Gabby figured someone had broken her eye socket as well.

"I told him no. Over and over, I told him no. He just kept trying to get me to touch him. His dick, I mean." She asked her what had happened. "I don't remember right now. But I told him no. I fought him off like you told me, and he ran off."

Paul just shook his head when she looked at him. "Hailey, the men here want to take you into the hospital.

I've sent for your daddy and told them not to allow him to drive."

"I kept telling him no, Aunt Gabby. But he kept hitting me. Harder than when he knocked me against the car window the first time." Gabby could tell her jaw was broken, or at least in terrible shape. Hailey was holding her jaw tight as she spoke to her. "He just kept hitting me and hitting me."

The medics moved in when she stepped back. Them pulling her from the car had her nearly pulling her gun out and killing them for making Hailey scream, but Paul was there to hold her back. Even as they laid her on the gurney, Gabby could see there was more damage done to her than just what she could see on her face.

As soon as they gave her something to knock her out, the medical team did an assessment of her injuries. They were vast and painful looking, to say the least. As soon as Harry was out of the car, he came running to where they were. It was all she could do to hold him back while she told him she was still alive.

"What happened to her?" Gabby told her older brother what she knew and what she'd been told by Hailey. "I thought she was home. I asked Rose where she was when I got home, and she said she was in her room. Then when the cop showed up, she wouldn't even speak to me. This is it, Gabby. I can't have her treating Hailey like this. Not anymore."

"Keep your voice down." He looked around when

she did. "Do you want everyone running back to her with what you're saying? Christ, Harry."

He started crying when he got to the gurney to look at his daughter. The two of them spoke quietly while the medics told them what had happened to her. While they were working to get her in a position to move her, she went to the other side of the car to look at the dead body.

"She didn't kill him. I mean, she had something to do with it, but she didn't kill him." Paul showed her what he'd been able to see that she couldn't in her position standing by the body. "He got the shit beat out of him too, it looks like. But the only thing she said to me when I got here was that he'd run off when she'd kicked him in his dick. It looks like he got out of the car to do whatever and fell on one of the frozen corn stalks. See here? It caught him right in the throat and severed the arteries. Bled out while she called us to come and get you."

"Have the parents been notified?" He said they'd not yet, waiting on making sure that Hailey got what she needed before anyone left here. "Good idea. Once she's on her way, have someone go with you. Wear your body cams too."

"I will. I know this kid, Gabby. I have to tell you, I'm surprised he's not been killed before now. Or killed someone else. He isn't the type of person that takes no as an answer. As you can see." She nodded and asked him if there had been reports from him before. "Ten at least. He's a twenty-two-year-old senior at the high school. His last year if I don't miss my bet."

"Are you serious? He's not graduated from high school, and they allowed him to keep going there? Christ." Paul told her who he was. "Why do I know that name? Chip Brunswick? It's not the mayor's son, is it?"

"His nephew. I think he's been staying with his uncle since the Christmas break. But he does live here. His parents have gone on a cruise or something. We were asked to go by their house a few times a day to make sure Chip here wasn't having any parties." She stood up when she'd seen all she could in the darkened area. "This is going to hit the fan, you know that, don't you? I mean, you being a cop, your brother acting judge on a major case coming up. People are going to have a field day with all this other shit too."

"I'm not going to work on this with you. But I would like to be kept in the loop, quietly if you can." Paul promised her he would. "I don't know if what I'm thinking is going to pan out or anything, but do me a favor and pull this kid's phone records and Rose's. I have no idea why, but I think she might well have planned this sort of thing. I could be wrong."

"You're never wrong when it comes to shit like this." He made himself a note. Paul was old school. He literally wrote it down on a small pad of paper rather than on his phone like most people did. She did the same thing, as he'd been the one that had trained her. "I'll let you know as soon as I do. Also, I'd like it if you had a burner so I can talk to you without anyone tracing it." She said she'd get herself one.

The body was taken away soon after the coroner arrived. Doc Massey should have retired years ago, but he was the best there was at his job. Being in his late seventies, the man didn't miss a beat. He used the newfangled equipment, what he called it, like the new kids on the block. He took one look at the car, then at the body, and nodded.

"Couldn't have happened to a better person if you ask me." He also didn't have a filter between his brain and his mouth most of the time. "I got me a couple of reports, Paul, that I'll make sure you get. Two other girls have been done in by this kind of shit. Who's the young lady? I'm assuming she made it."

"My niece." Massey looked at her, shocked. "Yes, she's been beaten up badly. The medics said she had five broken ribs on her right, as well as two on the left, broken right arm and wrist—a bite out of her ear. You might want to dig around for that while you're in there, Massey. If you'd not mind."

"No. I'll find it or know the reason why. How's Harry taking this? Not good, I'm betting." She said he was at the hospital now. "That Hailey is a good kid. She's one of the bravest kids I know, next to you, Gabby. Here's hoping she comes out on top of this."

The body was turned over, and she could see that his jaw was broken too. Not only that, but it looked like he might have had his hair pulled out in a few places, as well as what appeared to be nail cut marks on his cheeks. Just as Paul said, the stalk of corn, cut off at an angle when the crops had been brought in, killed him by going through his neck. The medics with Massey left it where it was when the body was turned over and put on the other gurney.

"They'll need to see what happened. I like a little drama when I have to show people how their loved one died. However, in this case, I'm thinking he wasn't loved all that much." It was Paul that asked Massey how he knew that. "About six months ago, I heard they were sending him to some kind of military place. To get his head on right. He'd gotten to be too much for him. Hell, I think he was too much for the two of them when they brought him home from that place. He's not theirs, and I'm betting every day they wish they'd not adopted him. As I said, I'll get you a couple of files I have that have his fingerprints and DNA all over the body. But old Fussy Ass wouldn't allow me to use them." Massey laughed. He sounded like a braying jackass when he was tickled like he was. "I had him sign off on it. For my eyes only, I told him. Hell, if that shit comes back to try and bite me in the ass, I'm going to show it to the queen herself if it'll get me out of trouble."

The cleanup wasn't anything she could help with, as she wasn't there in a professional capacity. Getting back in her truck, she let the thing warm up this time, thanking her for getting her to Hailey in time. As she sat there, she thought about what Massey had told her. Two bodies. Two young girls that had been killed by this kid.

Pulling into traffic, she headed to the hospital. Gabby also thought about how Rose was involved in this if she was. It would be just like her to have someone beat the shit out of Hailey so her daughters would be prettier. It was a sad case of the Little Cinder Girl all over. Except this evil stepmom was going to get her ass in trouble if she was even remotely in on anything that had happened here or in the last two deaths by Chippy.

The hospital wasn't busy this early in the morning. When she got up to the third floor where the operating rooms were, she found her brother still in his robe and slippers. She asked him if she needed to go get him something to wear.

"Birdy is going to find me some scrubs to put on. I want you to stay with me." Gabby asked if there had been any news. "Not yet. She was whisked away to surgery as soon as we got here. They were ready for her. She coded on the way in, Gabby. I don't know what I'd do if she were to leave me like this. Christ, I love that kid more than I do myself sometimes."

"I do too. She kept telling me she fought him off like I'd taught her to do." He hugged her, telling her he was so glad she'd talked him into letting her do that. "I know young boys and their parents much better than you do, Harry. They're all pieces of shits. You're the only man in the world I will ever love."

"You're hard on men, Gabby. I have pointed this out to you before." She was glad to see her brother smile at that.

The two of them were still waiting on news when their parents showed up. She didn't know who had called them but was grateful that someone had. In all the things going on tonight, she'd forgotten they'd moved to this town a few weeks ago to be closer to them. "The doctor is going to do his best with her. I know she's young and strong, so I'm hoping for the best here."

Harry didn't mention that she'd coded, and Gabby was glad. There were some things you didn't tell your parents, and she thought this was one of them. They weren't young, their mom and dad, and had seen a great deal, but no one wanted to know that their granddaughter had died once already tonight.

When it rounded up to six hours in surgery, Gabby found herself a quiet place to do something she told herself she'd never do and had told the other person she'd never call on her either. Reaching out into the cold dark night, she called for Gaea, the Mother to All Creatures.

"I felt her blood stain the ground, my child." Gabby cried a little, telling her what Gaea probably knew better than she did. "You know I will do whatever you wish. I owe you so much more than even this, helping a life for you."

"I don't want to tap you out, overwork your noddle here, Gaea, but I told you before, I was just in the right place at the right time, that's all." She nodded, as she did each time the two of them spoke. Gaea was the reason she was such a good cop. The older woman would help her with things when she felt the earth. "She cannot die. Hailey is the best part of her dad and my parents. I love her too, but I'm alone, and they will be should she pass away. Especially from something like this."

"The man, he is dead. It took me a moment to make sure the stalk was in the precise place when he stumbled onto it." Gabby asked her if she was being serious. "I am. Had I not intervened when I did, Gabriela, he was coming around the car to pull her from it and rape, then kill her. It was in his mind, you see, that she should have suffered a great deal. Be disfigured too. You would not have found the body either without my help. The deed wasn't finished until there was nothing left of her but a stain on the ground."

"Did Rose help him?" She nodded. "Was she fucking him? I'm assuming she was, because that sounds exactly like something she'd do."

"Fucking. It is a terrible word for making love. But in this case, you have gotten it right. They were fucking. Like little bunnies without a care in the world." Gaea smiled, but it was far from friendly. "I will help where I can. There are things in motion that will help you along with her as well. Do not be fooled by Rose's acts, Gabriela.

You know her to be evil, but she is so much more than that."

"I don't know what could be more evil than evil, but I'll take your word for it. I think Harry has had enough as well." She told her good. "You'll help her then? You'll make sure Gabby doesn't die?"

"Yes." She started to fade out but came back for a moment as a solid person. "She will no more die than you will, Gabriela Thomas." Then she was gone.

~*~

Pierce wandered around the halls just as he was told to do. There was going to be a reckoning here soon. Not really that bad, but it had to be taken care of now, or someone was going to be killed. The jail that was just outside of their little town, but still the one they used, was so run down, overpopulated, and in bad shape that he was surprised someone hadn't mentioned it before now.

"I've been taking pictures of the shit I'm finding. I might as well have been using a video recorder for as much is wrong here. What are you doing?" He told Madden he was measuring the walls. "I'm assuming it has something to do with the overall building?"

"There are codes that say how large a cell should be, and with that, how many people it can hold. The cells, according to the American Correctional Association, or the ACA, should be seventy square feet per prisoner. With overcrowding, they have been putting in a second bunk for an upper person." Madden asked him how large these rooms were. "Forty-eight. With three prisoners in the room when they're in a pinch. Which seems to be happening a great deal."

"Christ." Pierce agreed with him. "So we have these overcrowded cells, one shower stall for everyone to share, as well as the worst kind of conditions for the bathrooms. Demi is going to have a cow when she hears how bad this place really is."

"There's more. From what I've been able to find, there isn't a yard for them to walk in that's secure. So they've been having them walk around the commons area in a circle to give them exercise. Since the kitchens are in such poor shape, they're bringing in fast food that isn't fit to eat when they order it, much less when it travels all the way here in the back of a van." Pierce went over the list he'd been making since he arrived. "This place should have been shut down years, if not decades ago. I mean, just a few minutes ago, I had to go outside to pee. I was terrified of what would befall me if I were to have gone into that room." They both laughed, but he'd been really worried. He wasn't a little guy. "My bear curled up around me and seemed to be more afraid of going in there than he might have been on the darkest nights."

"I hear you."

They walked around for a little while longer together, then they parted ways again when they got to the next part of the building. Pierce was finding it hard to navigate through the halls. It seemed to him that someone had blocked off places that should have been halls and closed up rooms too. He was standing in front of what he thought should have been an office when he heard from Joey.

I'm going to go and see Margie now. I wanted to let you know so that if you feel me getting angry at her, you'll know the reason for it. He told her she'd do fine. *I do hope so. All I've been thinking about is how this is going to be coming to a head soon, and she'll be out of our life. Did you hear about the kids found not far from where you are in the jail?*

The girl and the boy out on a date? Yeah, the cops here are telling us that this little bitty thing of a girl beat this guy to shit, then lived to tell about it. I guess it was touch and go for her for a while, but she's going to pull through. She told him she was one of their nieces' age. *Yes. I can't imagine what would be going through my head if anything were to happen to one of my nieces. I guess the cop that works here part-time is her aunt. I've never met her, have you?*

No. Her brother is acting judge until Barker gets back from vacation. He'd not known that part. *Okay, I'm here. I have her things that I told her that I'd bring, and I'm going to make a big deal about how this is going to work out for her. Also, I've got a list of things I'm to ask her about. But not in an I'm-needing-more-information sort of way. Whatever the hell that means.*

He was still laughing about her when he stared at the door again. Or where the door should have been.

Looking around, he shifted himself to his big bear and slammed his body against the wall. Pierce felt it budge, and some of the drywall crumble, but it was still blocked. The voice behind him told him he should have been paying more attention than he had been.

"I tried that before. Not as a bear, but that is a good thing to use. I only got as far as using a reciprocating saw. As you can see there, I got it in before the whole place shut down because I blew the single fuse that covers here. Not a good thing to happen in a place full of criminals, I'd think." Turning slowly, he regarded the woman standing there. "Gabby Thomas. I'm assuming you're with the pretty lady in the office screaming at the mayor and the captain."

He nodded. While Pierce knew he could shift and dress at the same time, he wanted to get this doorway open. She asked if she could help him. When he nodded again, she came at him with her hand out. Pierce noticed that not only was it not trembling, but she didn't seem to care overly much that he outweighed her by about three hundred pounds.

Biting gently into her hand so they could talk, she asked him if he'd hit the wall again. After the third try, not only did they have the wall knocked down, but it showed him that there were several such doorways along this hall. They were on the fourth door when he heard from Demi.

I don't know what you're doing, but keep it up. You're

scaring the hell out of the men I'm in here with. They think I've opened up the gates of hell and am bringing the devil himself down on them. I love it. Pierce told her what they were doing and who he was working with. As his bear. *Good job. And so you know, Gabby needs to take this place over. The moron that works here thinks a good day at the office is not showing up at all. I'm about to go to prison for killing the lot of them.*

There are several rooms here, cluttered with boxes of things I've not had a chance to look into. Gabby is. But she is sort of just taking glances and mumbling a great deal to herself about penmanship or something. They look to me like old evidence. But then I'm not the type that would know anything about that. Also, these rooms look a great deal like classrooms, all the way to the chalkboards on a couple of walls. She asked him if she could find him easy enough. *I don't know why not. I mean, if I'm thinking this is laid out right, I'm right behind the captain's office. Or thereabouts. If there is so much overcrowding, why aren't they using these rooms for something other than collecting dust?*

I don't know, but I plan to find out. She said she'd be there in about half an hour and for him to find a place to shift. *You might want to tell Gabby to take off too. Someone has a real hard-on for finding her. She's in trouble about something that occurred last night. Apparently, she was at the scene where her niece was hurt, and the boss is giving her shit about it. By the way, you found the rooms like they are now. I don't want us getting into any shit about breaking down walls.*

Pierce told Demi about the accident and how her niece was hurt. After shifting and dressing, he told Gabby what was going on. She took off before he got a chance to thank her for her help. He had no idea where the thought came from, but he'd bet anything she knew more about these rooms than anyone did. And he'd bet she was able to get in and out of them without anyone noticing too.

Standing at one of the windows when Demi arrived, he was immediately asked what the fuck he was doing there. If not for Demi, he was sure he would have been arrested. He was also glad that not only had Gabby left, but he'd had the forethought to wipe up her shoe prints.

Chapter 9

The courtroom was filled to capacity. Joey was positive that most of the people there had nothing to do, so they showed up for some kind of entertainment. They were certainly going to get it. She had to smile when she thought of her conversation with Alden last night. He'd asked her how she was doing, and she broke down, telling him her sister was trying to pull a fast one on her.

"Are you planning on letting her do this to you?" She said they weren't. "They who, child? She's your sister. What would you do if none of this other stuff was going on? I mean, would you be leading her to the slaughter, so to speak, or just telling her no and getting on with your life? Because the way I see it, and I could be wrong, but she's still leading you down that path like she don't have a single care in the world. And you're letting her."

They talked about it with the family then. Meadow said Joey was only making her suffer for all the things she'd done to her. It wasn't as if they were doing this to catch a bigger fish. Margie was it. Besides Peter, and he was going to get his through the IRS. He'd not paid any taxes in the last fifteen years. Since Margie's name had been forged on all the other documents, he forfeited those to her, which was now all in Joey's name. Smiling, she thought of what the money from the two of them was going to be used for. The new jail would be a perfect reminder of how not to fuck with a family that not only had more funds than you did but was much smarter all the way around.

As the room was called to order, she looked around at her new family. Becky was even there, wanting to make sure everyone involved knew the little girl was safe. The things she'd been able to take from the house the night she and her mom fled were going to put Peter and Margie both behind bars for a very long time. The sentencing for Peter would be added to his tax evasion time.

Peter was to be brought out first. The police had told them they'd have extra men on duty for this. They were worried that Peter could have called in some extra muscle to get himself out of here. Not so much muscle, but people who owed him. Now with the primer to unlock the codes, they were able to see not only see who owed Peter but what he'd done with the body or bodies when they'd taken care of it for him. It was going to be a very high profile case when it hit the courthouse. But for now, they were working on his taxes. Mr. Shoe was excited to be taking care of both cases.

"I'm thinking we need to have our own seats in here for as much as we come to court for one of the family." Cindy told Pierce to hush, but neither one of them could stop laughing. "At least a little padding wouldn't go unnoticed."

As things got under control again, everyone was seated. Peter was brought out of the side door. It shocked her to her core at how much the man had aged while being in a jail cell for just three nights. They'd put him there when it became apparent he wasn't going to be able to get a loan for the amount of back taxes he owed, and since nothing was in his name, he didn't have anything to put up for sale to get it. Joey hadn't understood why he was still getting taxes charged against him since he didn't own the things, but Demi told her the money had come from somewhere. And since Margie had never worked a day in her life, it was solely his responsibility to pay taxes on his income, wherever it came from.

Peter asked if he could speak before the trial began. The judge told him he could, but there would be no grandstanding in his courtroom. He had enough on his plate today as it was. Judge Thomas, brother to Gabby, looked as worn and haggard as Peter did.

"Yes, sir. My girlfriend only needs to sign the paperwork for me to have rightful ownership of the things I erroneously put in her name. Once she does that, I'll have enough money to pay the fines, which I'm to understand have to be paid first, then I can set up a payment plan for the outstanding balance." Judge Thomas asked where his girlfriend was. "Jail. She tried to burn my house down around my ears a few weeks ago. She's coming to see you next."

"You keep some pretty interesting company, Mr. Hightower. Let me look at what I have here for a moment." Judge Thomas looked hard at the paperwork in front of him. She knew exactly what he was seeing first. Since he'd not moved anything else around, Joey knew he was looking at the birth certificate of her sister. "How long have you and Ms. Matthews been dating, Mr. Hightower?"

"Oh, let me see. I guess it would be about ten or so years. At least that long." Thomas asked him to repeat himself, to be sure of the time it had been. "Yes, she was a little young when we started out, but I have to tell you, she was nothing like any of the other women I dated."

"Do you realize that ten years ago would have made Ms. Matthews fourteen?" Joey stood up then, and the judge turned to her. "Do you have something to add to this, Mrs. McCray? I'm to understand you're sisters with this man's girlfriend."

"Yes, sir, she's my twin. My father passed away when we were twelve, and that is when Peter started his sexual affair with my sister." The room gasped, and she stood her ground. If anything, the judge looked sickened by what she was telling him. "The two of them have been having sex since then. I would also like to point out that in that paperwork you have there, it says Margie has had five abortions, as well as three miscarriages. Since the clinic where she had them performed is state funded, they take any DNA from the fetus for future reference. All of them were children of Peter. The first one, you can see she was barely thirteen years old."

Everyone in the room turned toward Peter. Judge Thomas had to bang his gavel hard several times before he could regain control. He looked at her and asked her what she wanted to do. Her mother stood up then and said she'd not known about the abortions but would very much like to press charges against Peter for the rape of her daughter.

"She can't do that." No one said anything to Peter as he ranted about how Margie was a willing participant in all the things she'd done with him. That was what Alan had been hoping he'd say. Winking at Joey, he waited until the judge got Peter to sit down and shut the hell up. "She knew about us being together."

"I knew they were together. I did. But since Mr. Hightower is a known homosexual, I only thought they were seeing each other in an older man sort of thing. Like her father figure." Mom asked if she could give Thomas something. The man was so poleaxed that he was nodding even as Mom walked up to hand him the paperwork. "You can see right there that Peter lured my daughter away from us with promises of a better life. Also, more money than she could ever spend in a single lifetime. He had her—well, performing, I suppose you could say, for others. He also paid for her to have lessons in shooting, as well as other means of killing someone. According to my daughter's diary that she left behind when she moved out at sixteen, you can see that she has murdered for him for a long time."

Judge Thomas looked over the pages of the diary as the courtroom got louder, accusing Peter of all sorts of things that were more than likely true. Finally, the judge asked for everyone to have a seat. He would return shortly. As he was leaving the room again, he looked at Joey.

"Come with me, Mrs. McCray."

She moved toward him to see what he wanted. Then he called in Mr. Shoe as well. The two of them were sitting in the room when the judge finally sat down.

He looked at her. "I can't do this trial. I can sit in on this today, but this is just more than I think I can handle with what I have going on at home right now."

"I understand. I read about your daughter in the paper this morning. She's a very brave young woman." He nodded, then looked at the paperwork he'd brought into the room with him. Thomas looked at Alan.

"I've known you all my life, Alan. Even before I knew to be afraid of you. So I can safely say I know you well enough to think you have a plan in all this. We both know he won't last a day in prison. Not for the tax evasion charges, but the molestation of a child. And it's right here in black and white that he did." Alan told him he did indeed have a plan. "Whatever it is, I'm all for it. The sooner this monster is off the streets, the better I'll sleep at night. I need you to tell me what to do, and it will happen just the way you want it."

"I was hoping you'd see your way fit to put him in the general population of the prison system, with everyone knowing what he was there for, pending trial for the charges being pressed against him by the child's own mother. I think it will take time for someone to gather him a defense pertaining to these things coming out. What do you think?" Thomas made himself a note and stuck it to the folder. "Also, as mentioned, Margie Matthews will be in soon. She's about the worst kind of monster there is. She might try and scam herself a better deal by saying she'd been lured away from her secure home. And how she was misled by Hightower. But the things she's done...well, let's just say getting the monster's spawn off the street will make a great many people sleep better tonight."

"I have a reference here. Let me look and see what it's about. I'm to understand there is a child involved as well?" Alan said that right now, she was staying with her Aunt Joey. "It's about the three bullets that were taken from the body of Rebecca Hightower. Wife?"

"Yes. I hadn't realized she was shot three times. When we had her body picked up and taken to the morgue, we didn't say anything to anyone for fear of bringing Hightower's wrath down on this town. The little girl, you see, she stole his book." Thomas asked about the book. "The FBI has it now. Since they broke the code a few days ago, they're digging up bodies right and left. It says in this book who did the killing. Margie did a great many of them, even as a child."

"According to this email I just got, it says the bullets that killed Rebecca had two sets of fingerprints on them. One was your sister's, Joey—the other Hightower's. It also said that there was DNA on it. They think he perhaps had kissed it before it was loaded in the gun. Christ."

She agreed with him but didn't speak. She wasn't even sure what she could have added to the conversation at this point.

"There is also the matter of the money. I'm to understand there is a great deal of it."

"It's been signed over to me." Thomas laughed and asked her how she'd managed to get that taken care of. "She thinks I'm going to do everything in my power to make sure she gets out. The story of being lured away and how Hightower made her do things is something that she's been playing me with for the last couple of weeks. I know better."

"Good for you, young lady." She smiled back at him. His was a sad and pain-filled smile to her. "My daughter is in bad shape. The man that hurt her, he's been going to high school, and he was twenty something years old. He beat her nearly to death. There will be a long recovery to her getting better. But I'm so worried she won't be the same little girl she was before. She didn't trust well. My second wife shook that right out of her. Why I married Rose, I don't even know anymore. But if you can find it in your heart to say a little prayer for my Hailey, I'd really appreciate it. I know she would as well."

"We'll all keep her in our thoughts and prayers, Your Honor." He nodded and asked them to go have a seat but to not say anything to anyone. Alan was out ahead of her, so she turned back to Thomas. "If you need anything, anything at all, you give one of us a call. We have powers and magic that will help the three of you. I've yet to meet your sister, but I'm to understand she's a ball-buster too."

"You got that right." He laughed. "Yes, I might just give you a call sometime for nothing more than someone to vent to. I'm so very grateful for what you've done here for me today. It will make my job so much easier."

As soon as she was seated again, Peter turned to look at her. He was smiling at her like that was going to make a bit of a difference with how she felt about him. For some reason, she had a feeling he'd been responsible for more deaths than were written down in the book. He'd only been keeping it updated because Margie was doing it. Joey just stared at him until he turned away when Judge Thomas came into the room. Whatever had happened from the time she'd left him until now, it had made him look fifty years younger. And a good deal less weighed down by life.

"His daughter is awake and asking for him." She thanked Demi. "No worries there. I was as glad to hear it as you are. Is everything set up?"

"Oh yes. It's going to be a nice little surprise for not just Peter but my sister as well." She looked over at the other woman. She'd been more than generous with not just her time but everything since Joey joined the family. "We need a girl's day out. Someplace fun and warm."

Demi was still laughing when Peter was asked to have a seat. The judge leaned toward his bailiff and spoke to him. For the next fifteen minutes, Thomas said, they'd be in a holding pattern. Yes, she thought, Peter and Margie were going to be blown away by what sort of backbone she'd gotten since they'd been children.

~*~

Pierce didn't like this. Something was going to blow, and he was terrified that one or more of the family was going to be hurt. They couldn't die any longer, but being in pain would be almost as bad, he thought. Watching the door as it slowly opened, he held onto Joey's hand while her sister walked in.

Yesterday Joey had gone to see her sister, taking her something to wear to the courtroom that wasn't drab orange. It wasn't a color he would have thought of being called drab, but that was what she called it, Joey told him.

The dress she was wearing looked like something

an older woman would wear. Even with her hair pulled back in a tight ponytail at the back of her head, it didn't dimmish the look of being someone much older than he knew Margie to be. He didn't understand that. Pierce thought that having her look young would have been the ticket, but this hadn't been his call.

Margie was obviously confused to find Peter still there. They were set next to each other, their hands chained to the table in front of them. They were trying their best to ignore the presence of the other, but even Pierce could tell they wanted to touch. It really sickened him when he thought of all the things he'd read in Margie's diary. The woman was as perverted as Peter was.

Judge Thomas looked around the courtroom for several long moments before he spoke directly to Peter and Margie. No matter what was said here today, Pierce couldn't wait for this to be over so he and Joey could get some serious downtime.

"Over my years as an attorney, I've met all kinds of people. You two are by far the most colorful. Right now, because I've just gotten some very good news, I'm going to allow you to speak. There will be no interrupting the other while he or she is talking." He looked at Margie. "Ms. Matthews, this will be your one and only shot at convincing me to let you off with time served or have you go directly to prison. The evidence against you is vast. The amount of it surpasses anything I would think even the best kind of lawyer would have been able to find. You have ten minutes to plead your case."

"I'm not sure what I could say here. I mean, I've been talking to my sister, and she and I have a plan for my getting my head on straight after—if I can get out from under this trouble I've gotten myself into. But I will tell you that when my daddy died, I was alone. Adrift, I guess you could call it. My mom and Joey had their own grief, and I felt as if there wasn't enough room for me to be there too. Peter Hightower came along, and I thought he was going to help me. But after talking with my sister, Joey, I realized he was just using me. For terrible things." She started crying then, and Pierce wanted to tell her no one believed her faking this right now. "He took me from the security of my home, even going so far as to get me out of school when my mom didn't know about it. Mr. Hightower promised me riches and pretty things. I mean, what little girl of twelve wouldn't want that sort of thing? But he did things to me, and I never saw anything more than him encouraging me to do more things for him."

"You said he took you from school? How many times would you say this happened? And how many times did your mother know about it?" Margie told Thomas her mom never knew about it, and at least two to three times a week. "You've been having this affair with this man since you were nothing more than a child. Why would you think anything he wanted to do was right? Did your parents ever talk to you about male predators?"

"Mr. Hightower was just there for me. I didn't

understand that what he was doing to me was wrong." Peter snorted, and Margie showed her true self for just a second. It was a horrifying look too. "See what I mean, Your Honor? He had me wrapped around his finger so I'd do just about anything he asked of me. He was—I guess you could call him my hero."

"Is he your hero now?" She shook her head and looked back at where Joey and Lauren were sitting. She told the judge while looking at them that she was looking forward to starting over as a family again. "I see. Anything else, Ms. Matthews?"

"No. I don't think so. Oh, I would like to thank my sister for all her help in this. She's been my rock throughout the entire thing. She's made me see what a terrible life I was leading. She even convinced me that had I stayed with Mr. Hightower longer, I might well have become a monster, as he is."

"Mr. Hightower, you may have your say in this." When Peter just sat there, Pierce wondered what he was going to do. Judge Thomas just waited as if he had the entire rest of his life to wait for what the older man had to say. "Take your time, sir. I know this is putting you on the spot."

"She's making out like she was some sort of saint in all this, far from it. It's an act, don't you see? She isn't going to change her ways any more than I'm going to become a straight man. Yeah, I said it. I'm a gay man trying my best to live in a world where we're not accepted.

But Margie isn't telling you the half of what she's done. She killed the same as I did. She even murdered my wife. Yeah, I asked her to do it, but she took a lot of pleasure in it." Judge Thomas asked him if he was making a confession or was he just ranting. "I guess you can call it a confession. I know I'm not getting out of prison in any way but a body bag. I found out this morning that I have that gay man disease. I'm sure as I'm sitting here a dead man, no matter what I do after today. You have that book she kept secrets in. I didn't think about how incriminating it might become. I would let her do just about anything she wanted in order to get her to do things for me."

"Shut up, you old fool." Margie tried to stand up. "Why are you saying these things? You did this to me."

"No. You were killing before I got to know you. It's what made me do the things I did to get you to come to me. Sir, if you'll look in the back yard where they lived, you'll find the body of their paper boy, as well as another grave that holds one of the many cleaning ladies at the house. Margie killed the boy when he told her she wasn't pretty, not like her sister. The maid, or whatever she was, lost her life when Margie here pushed her down the stairs when she wouldn't give her some money from her own purse. I believe you'll find the said purse, devoid of any money, with the woman."

Margie lunged at Peter, but since they were both chained, all she managed to do was break the chair she'd been sitting in, as well as knock Peter to the floor. There were several tense moments while they tried to upright the mess. However, Peter didn't get up.

The courtroom was cleared except for Pierce's family. He wasn't sure why they had been singled out. Peter wasn't related to them by any means other than Becky. So when he heard Margie screaming, he knew the man was either dead or close to it.

"Why was he saying these things? Why are you telling these people this?" Margie looked around and spotted her sister. "Help me, Joey. Help me make this right. The things he said to the judge are going to make it harder for me to get out and stay with you. You still want me to, don't you? I need to get out of jail, so I can assume the life I was meant to have."

"What life is it you think you were meant to live, Margie?" She told her they were going to be sisters. "We always have been sisters. We have been since we were born. But you seemed to have forgotten that over the years when all you wanted to do was ruin me. You might think you've fooled me, but you haven't. Once a monster, always a monster, if you ask me."

"But you said you'd help me." Joey told her she had, a great deal. "You mean because you got me a few good meals? Brought me in some underclothing? That's not what I want from you, Joey. You have to suffer as I have."

"Why?" Margie was off Peter now and standing up as well as she could while talking to Joey. "How is it that you've suffered? You could have been so much more than you are now had you just gotten your head out of your ass and given one thought to the people you were hurting. Peter was right. The two of you are exactly the same. The only difference between the two of you is that he's not going to be around as long as you are to really learn what suffering is like."

"You have my money. I helped gather that money up, and you're going to sign it back over to me right now. I made a mistake in doing that. Do it now, Joey, or so help me, I'll make you pay some other way." She told her what the money was going for. "For a fucking jail? You're going to take my money and build a jail with it? You fucking cunt. I had to kill a great many people to help my Peter get that money. We were going to be married. Have such a wonderful life."

"Peter is a gay man, Margie. I'm thinking he's had second thoughts on marrying you too. He didn't sound all that keen on having you around him anymore." Joey looked at Pierce and smiled. "Isn't that the impression you got from him? That he had washed his hands of Margie?"

"I did indeed."

The medical team showed up, and Meadow told them what Peter had told them about him having AIDs. Pierce got a little closer to the man on the floor and realized he was dead. It looked as if when Margie went after him, his head had been knocked hard enough against the floor to have caused a deadly head wound. The world wouldn't mourn the loss of this person. Pierce told Joey, who relayed it to her sister.

"No. He's not dead. He's my lover and friend." Pierce looked at Lucian when he said his name softly. This entire confession and all was being recorded. And if he remembered correctly, Margie had not only confessed about killing but that she'd profited by killing too. Her plan was yet to be revealed as she spoke harshly to Joey. "You have never been anything to me, you sap. Christ, when I think of all the shit you poured out to me while we were talking. I'd have to go back to my cell and nearly vomit the way I was working you. You believed every bit of it too. I'm going to get out of here, and I'm going to hunt you down, Joey. See if I don't. And I'm hoping I can find you with children. I will take great pleasure in making sure you watch them suffer as you've made me the last few days by being so sweet and loving to me."

"I never believed you, Margie. You can take that to the bank. Having you sign over all the money to me, that was brilliant on my part, I think. I mean, the town is going to get a new jail, just so the likes of you and Peter are never out and about with honest, caring people." Joey laughed, and he couldn't have been prouder of her. "I think we'll call it the jail given to the city by dumbasses. That's it. Dumbass Jail. It has a nice ring to it, don't you think?"

"That's enough." Judge Thomas told the attendants

that had come with Margie to take her back to her cell. After the medical team had gotten their protective gear on, they began to work on the dead man on the floor. It was over even before they began. "I'm going to charge Margaret Matthews with the murder of Peter Hightower. Adding to her sentence at this point would be just another way for her not to ever outlive the length of the sentencing she'll get."

They were home by nine that night. No one had really wanted any dinner, but they had already decided to eat out. By the time they were served their appetizers, each of them seemed to have caught their second wind. Even Becky, who had been very quiet through this, was eating better than he thought she had in a few days.

Pierce did wonder what was going to happen to the little girl once this was over. She had been staying at their house at night, but mostly she'd been spending the day with her grandmother or with Ian's children. Whatever she wanted, they would work together to make her feel as welcome as they had anyone else that had joined their family.

"I'm going to adopt Becky." Lauren spoke to him from across the table almost as soon as their dinner plates were carried away. "I've decided she'll be with family, and we're going to live close enough to all of you, so she also has support when she needs it. The kids, they stick together, don't they?"

"They do. And it's funny you should have said that

just now. I was wondering what her role in this family was going to be." Lauren nodded and smiled at him as Becky talked to his mom. "She's going to be all right, you know."

"I do. I've also spoken to Alan. He's going to make sure some of the money in those accounts is hers for college or whatever she needs. Joey said she'd help us along with rent and the like. I think I'm going to sell back my part of the business and learn how to be a grandma. I've not had an opportunity to do that yet. Are you working on it for me?"

Pierce laughed. "We are. Several times a day." That had the desired effect, and Lauren's cheeks pinked up. "We do plan on having children, but we've sort of been a little distracted lately. I'm thinking now that Margie is going away and Peter is gone, we'll have a little more time."

"Good. See that you do."

When they were walking out to their cars later that night, his mom hugged him. Then before she could get away, he pulled her to him and hugged her back.

Neither of them said a word. Mom moved on to the car that she and Dad had come in. He went to the one that he and Joey were driving. On the way home, he thought about the first thing he was going to do tomorrow, and that was going to be knocking down the walls at the police station. He had a feeling there was more to this than just some rooms being closed off.

Chapter 10

Gabby held onto her brother's hand as the surgeon told them what he'd done to make sure there wasn't any permanent damage done to Hailey. Mostly it was to her face, but her entire body had been beaten badly, he told them.

"She's in recovery now, which I have to say surprised me somewhat. But I also know Hailey was in good shape and that her being young played a big role in her coming out of the coma so well." Harry nodded. Gabby knew why she was out of the coma but hadn't told Harry. She wasn't sure if she ever would. "I know you've heard this list before, but I want you to know the extent of her injuries. The only reason I can think she's lived through this is the reasons I said—being young and in good health. Harry, she's going to need a lot of physical therapy as time goes by. Not just to walk, but to use her right hand."

"You said it had been broken." Doctor Montrose said that it had been crushed. It appeared to him that it had been crushed by the glove box over and over before she'd been able to free herself from it. "She's been taught by the best on how to take care of herself. If not for Gabby here, she'd be dead, I'm thinking."

"By all accounts, she should be." Both of them knew that. Even before Gaea had gotten to her that night, Hailey had coded again. It was only magic that had kept her from staying dead. "You should thank your sister daily for what she did. You're right. This would be a different scenario altogether without that. As I was saying. She had a crack in her skull that concerns me a great deal, but her memory and skills at recalling things are still intact. I would say her head was banged against the closed window on her side at least ten to fifteen times before it was stopped. Her jaw is broken as well but has been wired closed to heal. I think the fact that she was able to speak that night shows again how resilient the young are. The left ankle is broken but set in a cast. Eight ribs are broken, another three are cracked. Her right lung is healing, as well as the damage that was done to her liver. I'm thinking that with her broken hip, she was jerked against the lap belt with enough force to have sliced into her leg and displace the bone enough that it cracked under the pressure. She'll walk, but it might be a long time before she can do so without a limp."

He went on to tell them of the cuts and the number of stitches that had to be used to put her back together. Her eyes were still swollen shut, but he said that was a good thing. It had protected her eyes from whatever damage might well have been done to them. She was going to live. That was all she was going to let herself think about now. And the last words Gaea had said to her as she left that night. They would never die.

When her brother poked her, she looked around. They were alone again, in the room they'd been using as a place to rest and to gather themselves together. He asked her where she'd gone.

"I don't know that I could tell you what I might have been thinking about." He told her he'd been feeling the same way for the last couple of days. "Did you get the locks changed on the house? And an attorney for you?"

"I did before coming in here yesterday. On both things. Rose had taken her daughters to the zoo. She couldn't be bothered to come here to see my daughter, but she could go to the fucking zoo? Doesn't she know it's like twenty-five degrees outside?" She cocked her brow at him. "All right, I'm better now. Anyway, I changed the locks, hired that pack like you said, and have an off duty hanging around the house until further notice. Do you really think she hired Chip to kill my daughter, Gabby? That is just so…I don't have words for it."

"I'm not the investigating officer, but she and him have been having an affair for the last year and a half. They called each other a total of fifty times right up until he picked Hailey up. Then nothing from him afterwards. She made four to his cell phone that we've been able to trace back to her phone." Harry asked her if she knew why Hailey was with the man. "You know her friend Jolie? Well, she had called Hailey to tell her she was on her way to get her. Asked her if she'd wait outside her house for her, as they were running late for the meeting with the other girls on the project they'd been assigned. There wasn't a date between Chippy and Hailey, but Hailey going to the library before it closed to get a start on the project that was due in a month. Sounds like her, doesn't it? Getting started on it the same day."

"Yes, she would have treated it like they were behind right up until they were finished with it. No last minute things for my girl." Harry asked her why she'd gotten in the car with him if she knew. "I mean, I know for a fact she didn't like him. She thought him a pest when he came around the house to do chores. I'm guessing now he wasn't getting paid with cash."

"Don't go there, Harry. You know, as well as I do, that'll only make you insane. Well, in your case, insaner. But no, she didn't like him." Gabby knew he wasn't going to like this next part at all. "Rose helped him get her into the car. The neighbor across the street had called the police and told them they thought someone was being kidnapped. When they arrived at your home about twenty minutes later, Rose assured them it was a little joke, that Hailey was on a date with a nice young man. He picked her up at about six-thirty, an hour before the library closed up."

"Why did it take until three in the morning before anyone knew anything?" She knew the answer to that as well. Gabby had been going to the office off and on for the last several days. Mostly to just hear something different than medical terms, the police ones weren't all that much different—but the smell was an improvement over the hospital—the information she was giving her brother from the reports copied for her every day. "I mean, that's a good eight hours. What the hell did he do in all that time?"

"She killed him sometime between ten and midnight. It's difficult to get a good reading, as the ground he was on was frozen. But that's about what Massey has estimated." Harry said it was still a few hours. "I'm going to tell you something that you cannot repeat, Harry. If you do, then it's all over. Got it?"

He nodded. "Is it Rose? Did she have more to do with this than just helping him get her into the car? She was drugged, wasn't she?" She slapped her palm to his forehead and told him to stop finding shit. "I can't help it. I just don't see that Hailey would have willingly gotten into the car with him."

"I already told you she was helped into the car, didn't I? Now listen. Hailey was being drugged. Over a long period of time too. Not only is Rose complicit in her being hurt, but it looks like she'd been feeding her arsenic for the last year. Little bits at a time, but that had nothing to do with the four hours." He let the tears fall as she sat there with him. The room was the only place she trusted to talk to him in. She went over it daily with the little extra that Gaea had given her some years back. "You know I have friends in weird places, right?" He nodded, then looked around. "Gaea told me she'd tried her best to intervene on Hailey's part by getting Chippy lost on the way to the cornfield he took her to. Once they were there, Rose was waiting on him. I have no way of proving this, so I'm just letting you know, so you watch your back. All right?"

"Does she know what happened while they were there?" Gabby nodded. "Do I want to know? Am I going to lose my shit once I find out?"

"You will. Suffice it to say that the two of them together are two of the sickest fucks I've ever heard of." He sat there for several seconds, then jumped up. Barely making it to the trash can, he threw up three times before he simply slid to the floor, looking up at her. "You have a little puke on your lip there, Harry."

"Fuck you." She nodded and waited for him to speak again. "They had sex right there where they wanted my daughter to die, didn't they?" She nodded again. "More?"

"Yes. Are you sure you want to hear it?" He said he didn't but thought that he should. "They put her on the hood of the car while they fucked each other over her. Not only that, but there was semen on Hailey that didn't come from Chippy."

"Christ." He was sick twice more when he told her no more. But she knew that in a couple of minutes, he'd be asking her for the details. "Who was it?"

"His uncle." Nodding, he stayed where he was. She knew this was hard on him. It had made her sick as well. All these people conspiring against a teenager for no other reason than she was pretty. "There is a new group of people coming into the station house. They're all bears. I've met one of them. Pierce McCray. I think you might have met some of them today in the courtroom. I'm thinking as soon as they get in the house, things are going to start coming to light. Like the back rooms."

"Do you still think they're using those rooms for sex?" She said she didn't know, but that was high on her list. "Why would they do that? In a police station, of all places."

"Why would anyone look there? I mean, think about it, Harry. What better place to make movies than to do it right there in the station house? The room Pierce and I were able to get into was window dressing. Nothing in there. Dust out the ass and all the windows were opened for anyone to look into. I'll get to the other rooms, now that I have help. Having a bear help means there aren't any fuses to blow that alert them that I'm snooping around again." He asked her if she was being careful. "Yes. More than I ever have been in my life. But I have to tell you that you need to be more careful than me. They'll get to you or Hailey to get to me. Don't let that happen. I'm begging you."

"I'll be on the lookout for them." She nodded. "You think I should start carrying a gun again? I know I told you it went against everything I believed in. But this isn't anything that I signed up for."

"Yes. And like I've told you before, Harry, shoot to kill, not maim. Hurt people are dangerous people, and they can come back. Kill them if it means you live." He told her he loved her. "I love you too. Please, you have to believe me when I tell you, this is going to be dangerous for everyone until we get this taken care of."

"I believe you." He finally stood up with her help. "You're stronger, aren't you? I haven't wanted to ask you this, but is Hailey—?"

"Yes. I asked for help with her." He nodded and hugged her. Gabby hadn't realized how much she needed him until then. "I've taken some leave time, but that doesn't mean I won't be in the loop. Stay with me. You can stay in my apartment rather than being cornered at the house. All right?"

"Yes. I like that. It's closer to the hospital too."

There was so much she could tell her brother. So much he needed to know. But for now, they were being watched over. Then tomorrow, she was going to meet with Gaea and figure out what she could do now that she'd not been able to do before.

~*~

Madden didn't care for the police chief. Nor did

he care for most of the people in the station house. They were lazy and pissed off that cameras that should have been put in place months or even years ago were being installed. He was Pierce's backup man, but he was also keeping an eye on the shit going on around them.

I've been thinking about a couple of things I'd like to run by you. He smiled when his mom spoke to him. *This is purely something I've been thinking of, but I'm not sure I can figure it out on my own. You've always been my most supportive child.*

I see. Who else did you ask before I became the most supportive? I'm thinking Lucian. She told him to behave. *What is it, Mom? I'm here for you.*

The jail that is being put in. Is it going to be larger than the one there? I'm looking over these blueprints, and I can't make heads nor tails out of it. It seems to me the place is about half again as big as I think they're using. He told her what Pierce had figured out. *That makes sense. I found some entries from the books I got from Meadow and the others. That jail wasn't built to be a jail at all, but a home for the homeless. I don't know where things changed around yet, but after a few months of building the home, someone got the idea to use it as a jail. To me, that seems like something you'd have to figure out from the beginning. You know, for security purposes.*

I don't know. But did you happen to figure out when this place was built? She told him what she'd found. *The late forties? That seems dangerous. I mean, we're talking decades of no upgrades or any kind of security for the place.*

Well, not only was the place built back then, but there is a building someplace that holds more evidence than what you found in that storage locker the other day. Mom asked him to wait, and she'd get him the address. *It says here that it's on Maple Avenue. The building number is blurred. It's four numbers, and the first one is a nine. I'd say it's not much in the way of a large building. The places along the area, I'm thinking, are just run down houses that need a good kick in the bottom to get cleaned up.*

Does it tell you what the building was built for? I mean, there couldn't have been enough evidence when it was first built to warrant the need for an entirely new building. She told Madden what the entry said. *So they were going to use this place as a hideaway for women that were hurt in some way. All right. Very forward thinking for the times, but was it ever used for that?*

Not that I can see right now. She said she loved this kind of sleuthing. *I'm going to see what else I can find. There is something afoot here, and I need to solve it. Oh, before I forget to tell you, I've filed my bid to get to be mayor, and your dad is gathering up people to help me campaign. I think I can make a good dent in some of the things that are going on without even leaving the house.*

Madden told his brother what he'd been talking to Mom about. And about the building she had found. Pierce told him they'd take a drive by there when they were finished up.

"It could be that the building or whatever has

long since been torn down or even used for housing or something." For some reason, Madden thought it was being used for just what it said, evidence. "I'm trying to be positive for a change. I just heard from Joey. Margie is going to prison for life without parole. And all the money and properties that had been signed over to Joey are now going to be used for the city, with the exception of what is set aside for Becky. The red tape, I'm to understand, for a corporation to build something like this is a nightmare. I guess Meadow and Mel are working through it."

"The adoption paperwork has gone through for Becky too. She is excited to be living with her grandma close to her aunt." That made his brother smile. "You're all sappy again. Do you suppose that ever wears off?"

"Christ, I hope not. I love my wife." As his brother came down off the ladder he'd been on, Pierce told him he only had two more to go. One of them was in the chief's office. "I'm thinking I'm going to run into trouble with that one. So be ready for anything."

They were ready, he supposed. Madden was carrying a gun now, and he didn't hide the fact that he was. Even Pierce was carrying one. They had come in by order of the state of Ohio to do this project. If anyone were to try and detain or stop them from doing their duty, they were told to shoot to kill. Madden thought the man was kidding when he told him that.

"I don't kid about shooting someone, Mr. McCray." He told the governor he was sorry. "Don't be. I'm just glad your sister-in-law was able to spare the two of you for this. I'm also looking into a few other things while I'm working on things here."

Without any trouble from the men, they set up the cameras in the last two places. No one here would have access to the recordings, but it would be manned all the time.

They were driving down Maple Avenue around five when they realized the building could have been one of a dozen homes and buildings in the area where Mom told them it was.

"None of them scream the year time frame. But that doesn't mean much. Put some siding on a home, and it will hide all kinds of things from a person." Madden agreed. "I say we get back to the house and see what else Mom has — Look there, Madden."

The man going in and out of the building was none other than the mayor. He was with two other people, both of them dressed in black. They were carrying what looked to him like boxes and also some camera equipment. Madden recorded what they were seeing on his phone while Pierce called Demi. She said someone would be there in five minutes, but for them not to engage. They didn't want to, so that was an easy thing to follow.

Within minutes not only had the FBI shown up, but SWAT was pulling in as they watched. While he hadn't any idea what was going down, he thought his mom was going to be mayor before the election. Things were surely moving in her favor.

Before You Go...

HELP AN AUTHOR

write a review

THANK YOU!

Share your voice and help guide other readers to these wonderful books. Even if it's only a line or two, your reviews help readers discover the author's books so they can continue creating stories that you'll love. Log in to your favorite retailer and leave a review. Thank you.

AWARD WINNING, BESTSELLING AUTHOR

Kathi Barton, a winner of the Pinnacle Book Achievement Award and a best-selling author on Amazon and All Romance books, lives in Nashport, Ohio, with her husband, Paul. When not creating new worlds and romance, Kathi and her husband enjoy camping and going to auctions. She can also be seen at county fairs with her husband, who is an artist and potter.

Her muse, a cross between Jimmy Stewart and Hugh Jackman, brings her stories to life for her readers in a way that has them coming back time and again for more. Her favorite genre is paranormal romance, with a great deal of spice. You can visit Kathi online and drop her an email if you'd like. She loves hearing from her fans. aaronskiss@gmail.com.

Follow Kathi on her blog: http://kathisbartonauthor. blogspot.com/